Bolan thrust hims of the speeding "bullet" train

"Hey, Tanaga!" Bolan yelled into the wind. "It's you and me—"

Suddenly Tanaga's partner came hurtling toward The Executioner in a low kamikaze dive.

Bolan remained in a crouch, and supporting himself with his arms, swung both legs out in a scissor kick.

He wrapped his legs around the oncoming *ninja's* neck, then closed them in a viselike grip. The assassin's neck twisted and snapped. His limp body slithered along the roof and fell into the slipstream.

Bolan watched as his assailant hit the track in an explosion of skullbone and brain. . . .

Also available from Gold Eagle Books,
publishers of the Executioner series:

Mack Bolan's
ABLE TEAM

Mack Bolan's
PHOENIX FORCE

MACK BOLAN

THE EXECUTIONER 53

BOLAN

The Invisible Assassins

A GOLD EAGLE BOOK FROM

W◍RLDWIDE

TORONTO · NEW YORK · LONDON

Dedicated to the *Nisei* Yankee Samurai
who, as Americans of Japanese ancestry,
served their country in the dark days
of World War II and played such a vital role
in achieving victory.

First edition May 1983

Special thanks and acknowledgment to
Alan Bomack for his contributions to this work.

ISBN 0-373-61053-X

Printed in Canada

War's a brain-spattering, windpipe-splitting art,
Unless her cause by right be sanctified.
                                    —*Lord Byron*

It is courage that raises
the blood of life to crimson splendor.
                                    —*Bernard Shaw*

Man's malice through the centuries has turned
mere fountains of blood into raging rivers.
We can only tame such a flood with
unremitting courage. The source of that courage,
my friends, is simply the need, the desire, the hunger
to do what is right.
                    —*Mack Bolan, The Executioner*
(from his speech at the leaders' conference, Stony Man
Farm)

Zeko Tanaga is the name of an infamous Japanese terrorist leader, considered second only to Carlos "The Jackal" in the annals of international outrage. Tanaga was with the Japanese Red Army before he became a *ninja* under the mobster family Yamazaki. He was involved in the massacre at Lod Airport. Tanaga was supposedly killed in a training exercise in a terrorist camp in South Yemen.

1

MEN COULD DIE HERE.

Mack Bolan shifted his position, taking care not to disturb any of the charred rubble that was strewn across the floor. Jay Marten, his attention fixed on the street below, did not even hear the big man move.

Bolan sensed trouble. He automatically began to relax and then to tense his deeper muscle groups. He was readying himself for action, while on a more conscious level he strove to isolate precisely what it was that made him feel so uneasy.

He was standing well back in the darkest shadows, about eight feet from what had once been the window. At the window frame, silhouetted by the artificial glare of the street lighting, Marten was hunched low in the wide-open square, his elbows propped across the crumbled sill. Even before that first intuitive tingle subsided, Bolan picked his way silently through the trash on the floor and stood behind the other agent.

Neither man took his eyes off the road.

For Jay Marten, Colonel John Phoenix was a last-minute partner. Jay's boss had abruptly dismissed his protest that he did not need a nursemaid, with a serious caution that this time the orders came from the top.

Right from the top.

It could only mean that the subject of their surveillance, Kenji Shinoda, was in bigger trouble than Marten could venture a guess at . . . very big trouble.

Bolan tapped Marten on the shoulder and signaled that he wanted to use the Startron. Marten handed over the bulky nightscope, attached to his sniper rifle, to the man in black. Bolan rested his eye against the rubber cushioning ring and was slightly annoyed to find the scope needed to be readjusted.

He did not care much for Jay Marten. The younger man wore a button-down shirt and had a manner to match. He seemed like yet another ambitious college kid with a bent for snooping; but Bolan supposed he'd looked pretty good on paper to a hard-pressed recruiting officer.

Bolan was never tied down with red tape, and that was why he would always take the offensive—he was free to seize the initiative without having to fill out any forms in triplicate. So maybe it was simply the waiting that was making him edgy, and perhaps he was being unfair in his assessment of Marten. He would soon find out—when the action started.

And that built-in alarm system warned him it could start at any second.

He concentrated on the electronically reconstituted image of the deserted Los Angeles street. They had picked the best place possible for a stakeout; in fact, it was the only nearby place that could conceal them. The two men were on the second floor of an abandoned warehouse, torched twice within the last year by punks with nothing better to do. The entire block in front of them had been leveled months ago to make way for an auto-parts factory that had never been built.

The far side of Alvarez Street was flanked by a gray wall more than ten feet high, which now shielded only another few acres of wasteland. The whole area was a barren battlefield of recession-hit industries, funding cuts, shifting political priorities.

Bolan leaned forward far enough to make a quick check of Munsen Avenue, the cross street immediately below their observation point. It was as dead and deserted as the empty industrial boulevard.

He paused for a moment to scrutinize an abandoned filling station off to their left and a boarded-up hot-dog stand. It looked like the landscape of Hiroshima after the bomb—two or three structures inexplicably left intact amid the otherwise flattened ruins.

He wished there had been time to fully reconnoiter the whole area around Alvarez and Munsen. Bolan knew of more than one mission in Nam that had come to grief because of a lack of adequate reconnaissance. It had cost good men their lives, which was a lesson a surviving soldier would not forget.

"He's late," snapped Marten, double-checking his wristwatch.

"Is that what your file says—punctual?" Bolan asked.

Marten made no reply. He was not sure how seriously Colonel Phoenix was mocking him.

Bolan made another slow sweep along the wall. About two-thirds of the way down the block, one of the street lamps was out. It left a long gap of inky shadow in the otherwise garishly lighted street. Not that it made any difference to the Startron, a device whose business it was to probe the night.

Nothing moved in the darkness, but something was

wrong. It was empty out there, yet Bolan still sought to corroborate whatever primitive instinct it was that warned him of impending danger.

The best trackers in the Old West had an uncanny ability to read signs where no one else could even see the trail. It was not simply that they knew what to look for—a bent twig, a single pebble displaced, a scrape of mud—but what counted most was that they knew where to look. That was the real trick. Whether tracking a mountain lion or a man, they knew how their quarry thought and which route it would take as the fastest or the safest or the most deceptive.

Bolan's hunting instincts had first been sharpened in the swamps and undergrowth and fetid village alleyways of Southeast Asia, then honed to an even more lethal edge in the city jungles where he had waged his one-man war against the Mafia. He had stayed alive and had stayed fighting, despite incredible odds. He survived because the Executioner possessed that special talent for getting inside the minds of his opponents. One simple rule: know yourself, and know your enemy, and you can fight a hundred battles without disaster. That rule had insured continuing victories in Bolan's new terrorist wars.

Tonight Bolan was at a disadvantage. He had been on his way to a private demonstration of the very latest combat chopper, the Thunderstrike, a new breed of war machine, when Brognola's priority orders had intercepted him at LAX—Los Angeles airport. He knew very little about Kenji Shinoda.

"What have you got on this guy?" Bolan asked Marten, not lowering the weapon's sight.

"Ken Shinoda? A computer genius. He's sansei— third-generation Japanese-American. And one of the best cryptographers we have. He's worked out some of our toughest codes and then designed the systems to put them into operation. Ken Shinoda is the guy who invented the Checkmate program.''

Bolan pursed his lips. Marten could see he was suitably impressed.

''Isn't that why you're here, Colonel?''

Bolan ignored the question. ''How did your people get on to him?'' he asked.

''He's being considered for a transfer. They want him to head the Buzzsaw project.'' Marten hesitated as he turned back to check the street again. Phoenix should have known all this...but then, maybe he did. Marten suddenly suspected that he was being tested himself.

Bolan had indeed heard of Buzzsaw—an intelligence program that would use the very latest wrinkles in satellite communications and ultrahigh-speed transmission. He lowered the Startron. ''And that would mean liaison with other NATO members. As a cryptographer and programming genius, Shinoda was hitting the big time.''

''Right. So we were running a standard clearance. Just updating the file on him. Wasn't much to add. He and his girl had broken off their engagement last year. Then he made a couple of trips to the Caribbean and Japan. Anyway, we hardly had the tap on him when the call was intercepted. Whoever phoned him gave the instruction 'Corner of Alvarez and Munsen,' then he agreed 'Right—midnight' and hung up.''

Marten took the scope back while the big man stood and mulled over the reported exchange.

''That's all?''

"Yep. I saw the transcript," replied Marten. "They didn't stay on the line long enough to run any kind of a trace."

Marten had no idea which particular group of security agencies this Colonel Phoenix owed his allegiance to. He knew only that Colonel Phoenix had the power. It was not in any badge or plastic ID card, not even in the wicked Beretta 93-R he'd seen Phoenix check as soon as they had staked themselves out—no, it was an inner authority he possessed, which Marten had no choice but to respect.

Jim Garfield, Marten's boss, had made it quite plain: he was to cooperate fully, to defer if necessary to the colonel's judgment. To the young agent, it was all very irregular.

Right now, Jay Marten wished he could check with his partner, Hennessy, in the backup car, now under cover four long blocks away. Jeez, he hoped his buddy hadn't dozed off. But Marten could not break silence with Phoenix standing there, staring, his face a hardened mask.

"Is there any more on Shinoda?"

"He's well connected. Seems to know most of the people in his field," said Marten. "And he's known by them."

"How well liked is he?"

"Nobody that clever is universally liked," Marten observed dryly. "But he's respected all right. As I said, he works hard and plays hard. He enjoys the best R & R that money can buy. Likes to travel. But it looks as if somewhere along the line somebody got his hooks into him. And if he's susceptible to—"

"There's somebody coming." Bolan pointed to the far end of the street. "On foot."

At that long range the lone pedestrian was scarcely more than a ghostly flicker, but he was quickly approaching the first of the street lamps.

"I see him," confirmed Marten, watching through the Startron, which gave more than three times magnification. "Yeah, that looks like Shinoda. So...do you think the party we're interested in will actually show himself?"

"I doubt it—I think it'll be a drop."

"Then we might be in for a long wait to snatch whoever comes to collect the payoff."

Bolan hoped not, but Marten was probably right. "First of all, we have to see exactly when and where he makes the drop."

Shinoda, or whoever it was, just kept on coming.

Two...three.... Bolan internalized the pace, watching with his naked eye.

The man was approaching the unlighted stretch near the broken lamp.

Bolan quickly scanned the rest of the street. Still no one else in sight. No sign that a direct contact would be made.

Four...five....

The navy blue raincoat rendered Shinoda as just another shadow in the darkness.

Six...seven...eight.... Bolan continued monitoring.

Where the hell was he? An uneasy tremor snaked up the big man's spine, and this time it triggered an alarm bell in his brain.

Nine.... What's happening? Bolan grabbed the Startron from Marten.

The image was softly blurred. Out of focus, dammit: it seemed as if one figure was hovering over the other like some ghoulish night visitor draining his victim of lifeblood. Impatiently Bolan adjusted the focus. Marten looked at him sheepishly.

Now he could see clearly; now there was only one figure out there. Prone! Their subject was lying face-down on the sidewalk.

"They've got him!" Drawing his Beretta, Bolan ran for the stairs and descended them two at a time. He had no idea who "they" were, or how they had made the hit in the middle of an empty street. But he reviewed all the possibilities as, gun in hand, he raced across the intersection and up Alvarez Street.

Marten was right on his heels. He was shouting into the small transceiver: "Backup, backup! Close in—subject is down, I repeat, down!"

Shinoda was down all right—downright dead.

Bolan had reached the victim and was feeling for a pulse. Nothing. He checked the street in both directions. It was as lifeless as the corpse lying at his feet. Bolan holstered his gun.

"What the hell happened?" gasped Marten, squatting to inspect the body.

Bolan knew that a determined hit man would have used soft-nosed or explosive bullets—either way the killshot would have blown a crater in Shinoda. And yet he did not appear to have any wound whatsoever.

"Jeez, how am I going to explain this?" Marten wondered aloud. He looked up, hearing a car approach along Munsen.

"Right now, Shinoda would like to have your problem," remarked Bolan. He studied the street surface. He looked up at the wall five feet away. Whoever hit the computer wizard had got away. Bolan did not believe in magic. The only other logical answer was to have gone to ground—he had used the trick himself—so he began casting around for a manhole cover, a sewer entrance, anything large enough for a man to crawl down, to hide or escape.

A car wheeled round onto their street. As it cleared the far end of the wall, its lights swept the roadway. Bolan turned his back on the vehicle, checking for any telltale evidence revealed by the high-beam illumination.

Yeah, there it was—a circular steel plate about thirty feet away. He unholstered the Beretta again and strode out into the street.

Marten still crouched close to the body, bewildered by what had happened. He must make an immediate report on the car radio. He began to straighten up....

That car did not look like the beat-up Dodge that was working the backup detail. Marten tried to shield his eyes from the glare—it could not be Hennessy's car. It wasn't even slowing down.

"Look out, Colonel!" he screamed.

The car was roaring down the street toward them...aimed like a missile at Bolan.

2

BOLAN WAS ALREADY TURNING. Legs apart, arm extended, gun hand balanced by the other palm, the big man had only micro-moments to make his play. Shades of Italy, of the streetfight fought with guns and cars.

In the short distance from the corner, the sleek black Firebird with gold trim had accelerated with a powerful burst. Thirty-five hundred pounds of metal body and snarling engine were hurtling toward him at seventy miles an hour and climbing.

Bolan stood his ground.

The Firebird would cover that final hundred yards in less than three seconds.

Bolan aimed through the blinding intensity of its headlights, directly at the place the driver should be sitting. The windshield shattered into myriad cracks from the impact of the 9mm bullet.

The car veered to the left.

Bolan dived the other way.

It was too late to roll completely clear. The rubberized edge of the right front fender clipped his calf in midair and sent Bolan sprawling.

As he smashed onto the street, the pistol spun from his numb fingers and slid across the pavement.

The driver had anticipated Bolan's shot. He

straightened up as he wrenched the wheel over to propel the Firebird onto the sidewalk.

Bolan had caught the fleeting impression of a face: lips curled in a victorious sneer, eyes just slits of hatred. The driver was going to take them all out. No witnesses.

The car bounced over the outstretched legs of Shinoda's corpse. Marten had turned and taken two fast paces...but there was nowhere for him to run.

The black monster slammed into the young agent and smeared him along twelve feet of cinder-block wall. Over the sound of the straining engine came the tortured shriek of scraping metal and screaming man. Then the car fishtailed back to the street again and accelerated away.

Bolan had dragged himself to his gun, tried to aim, but there was not enough feeling in his arm to hold it steady. The shot was way off.

A second car was approaching.

Bolan shifted the Beretta to his left hand and awkwardly sat up as the Dodge skidded to a halt.

"Oh, my God!" Hennessy yelled as he leaped out. Marten's broken body lay like a discarded rag doll at the foot of the wall. The backup man ran past Bolan to check on his buddy. But it was pointless; he could not even recognize the crushed mess as Jay Marten.

Bolan climbed unsteadily to his feet. Nothing seemed broken, but he was sore.

Sore as in bruised and aching.

And sore as in angry.

As in mad.

Fighting mad!

"HOW DOES THAT FEEL?" Her fingertips were cool and soft against his skin.

In another place, in other circumstances, Bolan might have replied quite differently. This time he just gave a shrug.

She was young. With her glossy auburn hair and green eyes, she was very attractive. And Dr. Vicky Stevens was also extremely efficient.

"Does that hurt?" she asked, probing along the muscle.

Bolan shook his head.

"You've been very lucky, Colonel. Nothing seems to be broken. But we'll still have to wait for the X-ray results."

No, lady, I've been careless, thought Bolan, and that too made him angry. Angry at himself.

Blackmailers were not his usual line of business, and he did not like getting dropped into the middle of a local operation like that. But when some dirty little extortion scheme threatened to jeopardize the security of the entire United States, Brognola had no choice but to assign him to the case.

Bolan was not making excuses for himself. Getting caught off guard by a speeding car on a badly lighted street offended his own sense of professionalism.

Professionalism was not merely a question of remuneration for one's services, it was a state of mind: dedication and detachment born out of hard experience. Men like Jay Marten did not live long enough to get that experience. But Bolan had paid his dues. He'd had plenty of experience. Bolan was the consummate professional.

The slightly mocking smile in the emerald depths of Dr. Stevens's eyes did not help his mood.

She wasn't laughing at him. The intense presence of Colonel Phoenix prevented that. She was just trying to practice her own form of professional detachment. It was the defensive mechanism of a woman that made her smile.

He had quite a body. Phoenix certainly was not the usual kind of patient she attended here at the medical center. The tall man sitting on the edge of the examination table was in superb shape, despite the evident fact that his body had taken some vicious punishment in its time. She could only guess at what terrible retribution he had dished out to his foes.

For a few moments he had been lost in thoughts of his own, but now the colonel glanced up, and she awkwardly looked away. "Nurse MacLean will put a dressing over that scrape on your elbow."

Her tone made it clear she would not tolerate an argument. In the hospital, doctors were the ranking officers, even if they were young and pretty.

He watched her as she left the room. Her legs were pleasingly trim and the slight sway of her hips was not disguised by the shapeless white coat.

Bolan was left alone to pursue a frustrating chain of unanswered questions. The coroner's team should be able to come up with the clinical cause of Shinoda's death—that was the "what happened"—but it still would not explain the "how" of it.

How was it possible for them to blow a guy away without leaving a mark?

And just who were "they"?

That's where Bolan started. He was brooding over the why of it when Nurse MacLean appeared, carrying a gauze dressing and instruments in a steel dish. She quickly cleaned his arm.

If Shinoda was a blackmail victim, then surely they would not kill him off, reasoned Bolan. And in what way had this technological wizard laid himself open to blackmail in the first place?

The guy wouldn't have been caught with his fingers in the till; cash transactions did not figure in Shinoda's line of work. And fiddling with his expense account would hardly qualify Shinoda to have his arm twisted.

What did that leave? He was single. Bolan recalled that Marten had said he'd been engaged for a while. Okay, assuming that Shinoda led an average love life, what did he have to conceal? What would he rather betray his country for than have revealed? In this permissive day and age it was difficult to imagine what a normal bachelor would find so crucially embarrassing. Had he been seen in some sex show or brothel overseas? Had he been snapped in bed with a couple of hookers? Was he bisexual?

That wasn't enough.

Rumors of a person's sexual preference, or especially prowess, were more likely to prove an intriguing enticement than a subject for blackmail.

No, it did not add up.

"Keep still while I tape this," Nurse MacLean demanded crisply. Her manner was every bit as commanding as the young doctor's.

There was something else the young agent had said. "I read the transcript...." Hell, a transcript did not show the inflection, mood, intention in a man's voice. Shinoda may indeed have been receiving instructions for a meeting, but on the other hand the caller might have repeated an order that in fact Shinoda had given them. Shinoda himself might have been dictating the time of the meet.

"God, I hate having to make phone calls like that," grumbled the heavyset man who ambled into the room. He was Marten's boss, Jim Garfield; he was the one who had ordered Hennessy to bring the colonel in for a hospital checkup, a rare experience for a man usually served by the limitless resources of his own Stony Man Farm. Garfield held the door open for the nurse to leave, then turned back to Bolan. "I've just spoken to Jay's wife...."

Bolan could sympathize. He'd had to make more than a few calls like that, too. Death was no stranger to The Executioner; he was on intimate terms with it.

"I told her...well, I just said it was an accident."

Some accident.

Garfield stood there for a moment forlornly looking his age. He stroked his hand across the spiky top of his crew cut, a hairstyle he had seen no reason to change since Eisenhower had been president. He had started in this line of work right after Korea.

"So they patched you up?"

"Yeah, I'm okay," nodded Bolan.

"We found his car."

"The Firebird?"

"No, Shinoda's. A Jaguar X J S. It was half a mile away. On a supermarket lot."

That bothered Bolan. And why was Shinoda at the agreed location nearly fifteen minutes late if he was following instructions for a payoff? The more likely explanation was that Shinoda had been going there to *collect*.

Bolan was coming around to the conclusion that this codemaking genius was not the victim, but the blackmailer himself. "Do you have the original tape? I want to hear it."

"Sure, Colonel, it's at the office," Garfield told him. "I'll take you over there. But first I want to see if anything's been found at Shinoda's apartment."

"All right. Let's go."

The two men had almost reached the Emergency reception area when they were intercepted by a balding physician with a slightly mystified expression.

"Mr. Garfield!" The doctor signaled with the file folder he was carrying.

"Ah, Dr. Benson, what have you found out?"

"The detailed autopsy hasn't been completed, but the initial inspection didn't reveal much. No immediately visible wounds." Dr. Benson took advantage of being in a Smoking Permitted area to light a cigarette, then flipped open the file and glanced at it. "These are the first reports from the lab. No evidence of toxins.... Hmm, that's interesting...."

"What is it?" demanded Bolan.

"Sodium thiosulfate. It was in the sample taken from under the fingernails."

"So what's that mean?" asked Garfield.

"It's fixer," said Bolan. "Sodium thiosulfate is a chemical used to fix photographic negatives."

"That's right," Benson confirmed, puffing quickly at his cigarette. "He must have been an amateur photographer."

Suddenly Bolan very much wanted to visit Shinoda's apartment.

"We've still got to know what killed him," said Garfield. "What's your best guess?"

Benson only hesitated for a moment. "He seems to have succumbed to a massive neurological spasm. But how was it induced? I have no idea."

3

IT WAS A QUIET STREET, well tended and rich. The white tower of Westdale Heights, thirty-two stories of luxurious condominium apartments, rose amid its own private complex of tennis courts and swimming pools. A battery of lawn sprinklers insured that the grass was maintained as a lush carpet, which hidden floodlights now rendered an almost unnatural green.

Shinoda's apartment was on the eighth floor.

A uniformed cop stood guard in the corridor outside. Garfield showed his identification and vouched for Colonel Phoenix. The sentry jerked his head at the door: they could pass.

Despite the lateness of the hour there was already quite a crowd at work inside when Garfield and Bolan arrived. Bolan had been detained at the medical center long enough for a diverse team of experts to swing into action.

It seemed a lot of people were interested in the demise of Kenji Shinoda.

The local homicide captain did not like it that yet another respected citizen had been cut down on an L.A. street. The NSA boys were curious because the victim was one of the nation's top cryptographers. Hennessy was there watching a fingerprint team dust down the door handles. And two dour-looking agents from another federal department were trying to find out if they, too, should be concerned.

"As you can see, it hasn't exactly been ransacked," one of the detectives told Garfield, "but somebody's been in here all right."

"Nothing much seems to have been touched," added Hennessy, coming across to give his boss the guided tour. "I guess whoever they were knew what they were after."

Yeah, thought Bolan, *but did they find it?*

"That desk over there has been searched. And the filing cabinet has been rifled," Hennessy pointed out, "and if you'll come through here...on the right...yes, in there. See, he'd converted the second bathroom into a darkroom."

A police photographer took a final wide-angle shot of the trashed room and retreated to allow the two newcomers to inspect the place.

None of the equipment had been smashed. The enlarger stood in place on the Formica homemade top, a small print dryer was in the corner, and three empty chemical trays sat on a rubber mat along the bottom of the bath.

Scattered across the floor were strips of 35mm negative, each about a foot long, obviously dumped out by someone in search of a specific picture.

"Your being-blackmail theory seems to have run out of gas," said Bolan.

"It looks that way," Garfield concurred glumly. He had already received the report that nothing had been found on the body except a wallet and loose change: no wad of bills for a payoff. Garfield's hand once more brushed nervously across the graying bristle of his crew cut; he looked like a frustrated foot-

ball coach whose miscalculation had cost his team
dearly.

Bolan was not so easily defeated. Ever. He did not
care if the other side was a few points ahead. Now it
was time for him to roll up some yardage of his own.
Bolan would get to the bottom of this mysterious killing; somebody was going to pay for trying to turn
him into a hit-and-run statistic.

Garfield was inspecting two eight-by-ten black-
and-white prints. They were well-composed views of
a Shinto shrine. "He must have taken them on his recent vacation in Japan."

Bolan scooped up a couple more photos from beside the washbasin pedestal. They showed Shinoda in
a white karate suit halfway through a practice *kata*.
He looked a lot more lively and healthy than when
Bolan had last seen him.

"A regular Bruce Lee, wasn't he?" said Garfield.
"He must have had a friend take these when he was
working out at the Iron Fist Association."

Bolan gave the security agent an inquiring look.

"It was in his wallet. A membership card," explained Garfield. "He belonged to a karate and kung
fu club here in town."

Even more puzzling. If Shinoda was trained in the
martial arts, why had he been taken by surprise so
easily?

Garfield bent down and began to scoop up the cut
strips of negatives. There were about three dozen of
them. A policeman standing in the doorway looked
resentful that Garfield had interfered with potential
evidence.

"We'll send them on down to you," growled Garfield.

The cop knew better than to argue. One of his partners appeared. "The guy who runs the all-night convenience store on the corner said Shinoda dropped in about eleven-thirty."

"What time did *you* get here?" Bolan asked the cop.

"About one-thirty. Along with Mr. Hennessy, we were the first to arrive."

"See if there's anyone around who saw a black Firebird parked in this area between midnight and one-thirty," Bolan told him.

The cop looked at his watch with a frown. Was he supposed to go knocking on people's doors at this hour? He departed with a shrug.

As Bolan and Garfield returned to the lounge, the detective there came to speak to them. "This might sound crazy, because nobody passed us on the way up and there was a squad car outside, but I have the feeling we might have disturbed whoever was in here."

"Oh?" Garfield looked at him with interest. "What makes you think that?"

"The guy who just left said the top two drawers of the desk weren't touched. The intruder might not have finished the job he set out to do."

Bolan crossed to the long window in four strides even before the other man had finished his sentence. The latch was open on the sliding glass door. Bolan pulled it back and, drawing his weapon, stepped out onto the balcony.

It was nothing more than a concrete slab four feet wide by about twenty feet long, hemmed in by a metal grille guardrail. A puddle of water had collected under the back of the air-conditioning unit. The balcony was deserted.

Bolan looked over the edge. The sheer white wall

dropped smoothly to the flower garden eight floors below. An evenly matched row of similar balconies jutted out from each of the lower apartments. No utility pipes to mar the surface. No fancy brickwork. No handy ledges.

Garfield came out and peered over at the floodlit grounds. He stepped back quickly; evidently he did not have a head for heights. "Nah, you'd have to be a human fly to get down there."

Bolan was not ruling that out. He looked pensive as he stepped back into the main room.

"Colonel Phoenix?" A uniformed cop had entered the apartment. Garfield shook his head at the mis-identification and tipped his thumb toward Bolan. The patrolman turned to address him. "A call has just been patched through to say a Mr. Hal Brognola and your colleagues are on their way. They're flying in right now."

Bolan nodded. He could use some backup. Garfield's comment about a "human fly" still echoed in his mind.

"As soon as it's light I want you to have that wall out there examined," he said to the ranking agent. "And the one running alongside Alvarez Street. Inch by inch if necessary. See if you can find any unexplained marks. Anything at all."

"Okay." Garfield managed a weary shrug. It would be dawn soon enough. "Let's get back to my office. I could use a coffee. We can wait for your people there. Oh, yeah, and you wanted to hear that tape."

BOLAN SAT SLIGHTLY HUNCHED FORWARD, head cocked toward the speaker. It was the tenth time he had listened to it.

He hit the Stop button.

You could read it either way, he decided. Shinoda might have been repeating prior instructions or on the other hand he might have been issuing an order; his clipped tone was inscrutable. It was understandable that an overeager young agent like Marten, ambitious for a big-league bust, could have jumped to the conclusion that Shinoda was having his arm twisted, especially if he had only read a transcript of the two-sentence conversation. Still, it was a terrible price that young agent had had to pay. Somebody should have told the kid: it only takes one mistake. But Bolan would avenge him, that much was certain.

Finally conceding that there was nothing more he could get from the recording, Bolan stalked out down the corridor. It was quiet. Hennessy had signed out for the night. Garfield had gone for an early breakfast.

The door to Garfield's office was open. The duplicate keys to Shinoda's apartment were lying on the desk, alongside the half dozen prints they had found.

The couch along the far wall looked inviting, but there was no point in sacking out; Brognola and the others would be here shortly. And, Bolan hoped, they would bring some answers with them.

Steve Corbett was working in the cluttered laboratory at the end of the corridor. Bolan wondered what luck the technician had had; maybe those strips of negative would reveal something.

Corbett ran the all-purpose lab attached to Garfield's small secret service department. A tight budget would not allow anything more elaborate. Serious forensic investigation or detailed technical work were farmed out to the appropriate authorities, but Corbett and his assistant Larry Fisk could handle the more routine matters.

Garfield had called Corbett in early to work on the negs. He, in turn, determined he should not be the only one to suffer, and he had called Fisk in, too. Bolan found Corbett whistling as he peered through the microscope.

The technician looked up, still slightly sleepy-eyed but smiling. "Just about finished! I was matching the last of these cuts precisely."

There were a dozen blank sheets of paper lying in a row along the workbench counter; they were marked at the top Roll 1 through Roll 12. The pages at either end were empty. The rest were covered with carefully laid out strips of film.

"As far as I can see there were in fact only eleven rolls," said Corbett, placing the two pieces he had been studying on the bottom of the Roll 10 sheet. "Everything's black-and-white. He must have sent out his color films just like anyone else."

So whatever it was that Shinoda had photographed, thought Bolan, whatever was so incriminating, he had been smart enough to shoot in monochrome. That way he could process it at home by himself.

"Most of the cut pieces could be matched to their strips simply by eyeballing them and watching the edge numbers," continued Corbett. "A few I had to double-check under the microscope. Anyway, what you brought back is all laid out here."

"What happened to Roll 1?"

"Larry has those strips in the darkroom. I've got him making up contacts—that way it'll be easier for the rest of you to check them out. From what I could

tell, they begin with some pictures of a workout, judo
or something like that, then the rest are tourist snapshots taken in Japan. We'll be able to see better when
Larry's finished.''

"What about this hole here?" Bolan tapped the
gap in the middle of Roll 7.

"Those ones, Colonel Phoenix, appear to be missing." He bent forward and checked the edge numbers. "Ten frames, to be precise."

Before Bolan could ask more questions, Corbett's
assistant emerged from the darkroom. "Here's the
first roll."

He handed Bolan a single eight-by-ten glossy on
which was printed a series of tiny black-and-white
photographs, direct contacts of all the negatives from
Roll 1.

The first seven were of Shinoda and a couple of
friends in various action poses from a karate session.
The rest were of a Japanese city—Tokyo, probably—
a view from his hotel window, a temple and some
candid shots of street characters.

Bolan stared at them for several moments.

"See something?" asked Corbett.

"Would Shinoda have made up contact sheets like
this?"

"Quite probably. When you've processed a lot of
film you usually run off some contacts. If you've got
dozens of pictures, this would be the quickest way to
check which ones you wanted to pick out for enlarge-
ment."

Bolan turned away so suddenly he almost knocked
the film out of Fisk's hand. Corbett was surprised
that their guest had enough energy left to race down
the corridor that way.

He walked to the door to see what had got Colonel Phoenix so excited.

Bolan was ducking into Garfield's office, where he grabbed the keys from the desk.

"Your boss better get over to Shinoda's apartment as fast as he can," Bolan told the startled technician. "I know what the intruder was after. And if Hal Brognola turns up here, give him the address. Tell them to follow me!"

4

THERE WAS NO COP standing guard outside the door when Bolan got there. All the experts had gone back to their offices or back to bed.

It was quiet inside the apartment. Streaks of hazy dawn light filtered through the rough-weave curtains, which Bolan drew open.

There was little sign that a team of specialists had given the place the once-over, except for an odd mixture of butts in the large ashtray and a film of powder around the door handle and on the glass-topped coffee table.

Bolan drew the Beretta and went to Shinoda's desk, in an alcove in the main room.

It was a heavy rolltop desk, probably not worth all that much as an antique, but it had been nicely refinished. With one hand Bolan opened it. The desk was full of the usual paraphernalia but nothing that attracted his attention. What had that young cop said? The top two drawers....

He slid the first one out. Personal paperwork—insurance policies, bills, an outdated driver's license, a credit card application—lay on top of an old computer printout. Bolan felt underneath.

Nothing there.

He opened the second drawer. Some camera equipment. Filters. A telephoto lens in its box. He stroked his fingertips on the underside of the drawer. And that was where it was.

Shinoda really had been an amateur at this game. Bolan smiled grimly as he pulled out the eight-by-ten contact sheet. That's what had killed him.

The city detectives had been so busy checking for what might have been broken into and collecting possible fingerprints that they had missed the photographic print taped to the underside of the drawer.

"Roll 7, I'll bet," Bolan murmured to himself. There was not enough daylight yet to get a good look at pictures this small, so he switched on a floor lamp and, still gripping the gun in his right hand, picked up a small magnifying glass from the clutter in the desk.

The first few photos were of a traditional Japanese building. Shinoda had taken it from several angles. The shots along the bottom row were seascapes, showing two large rocks with a line or cable of some sort stretched between them. Bolan mentally filed the images for future reference.

The middle two rows were the pictures from the missing negative strips. Bolan slowly ran the magnifying lens over them.

The first two shots were out of focus. Three more were obscured by large blurred heads in close-up; Shinoda had been trying to shoot through a crowd. The remainder showed his subject clearly: a group of four—three men and a young woman, all Japanese— against a backdrop of evergreens.

Bolan studied the group more closely. One of the men stood a head taller than the others; he had the build of a wrestler, and there was something odd about his left hand. In most of the shots he appeared to be listening or talking to a younger guy wearing glasses. Bolan was not sure, but there was something about his haircut and the fit of his clothes that suggested the other man was a well-heeled American rather than a native Japanese.

Bolan inspected one particular picture under the glass. The big fellow had his left hand on the visitor's shoulder. It looked as if the top of his little finger was missing.

These contacts could be rephotographed and enlarged. All the details would show up nicely then.

A siren wailed in the distance. Must be Garfield coming on the run.

The third older man in the photographs with a dapper, studious look could be easily recognized: he had a strange streak of snowy white hair zigzagging through an otherwise full black mop. Bolan turned his attention to the woman.

A second far-off siren added to the city's dawn chorus. Brognola was on his way. And it would not be a wasted journey. Bolan had something to show them all.

He looked at the woman as closely as the magnifying glass permitted. Quite pretty in a serious, almost stern way. The men seemed to be paying little attention to her; they were focused on the guy with the spectacles. This woman looked average, with no distinguishing features. Again, they would be able to get a better view of her in the blowups.

He put down the glass and rubbed the bridge of his nose between his fingertips. Oriental faces...they haunted him.

The sirens wailed louder, then died as the cars drew

up outside the apartment block. Bolan's allies would be here at any moment.

Bolan looked up. He was still coming to grips with that half-glimpsed face of the hit-and-run driver. The vision of it had never left his mind. Those dark eyes, two malevolent slits, continued to bore into him.

Oriental eyes!

Reflected in the window....

Marten's killer was right behind him.

Bolan moved.

Knees flexing, weight shifting, he began to duck in a sweeping turn as the attacker sliced the Beretta from his hand, knocking it across the floor. Then the attacker's lightning-fast arms held Bolan's shoulder and left elbow in a tightening grip.

Bolan froze in mid-turn. The pain was excruciating. White-hot daggers raced up his arm, stabbing at his heart. His legs collapsed beneath him.

Even as the pain slammed the breath from his body, Bolan's mind was racing. He knew this guy. From somewhere in the past he dimly recognized him—and the big warrior was not going to let the bastard get him now.

His right arm flailed, circling until he wrapped his fingers around the upright of the lampstand.

It was an awkward swing back over his head, but Bolan managed to catch the killer across the side of the face with the teak pole. Shade, bulb and wire fixture were mangled. The numbing grip on his shoulder loosened.

Bolan took advantage of the momentary relaxation to jab the broken lamp savagely at his adversary's eyes.

The move forced a retreat.

For a few seconds the two fighters squared off, each remaining motionless. Bolan's every sense was attuned to the slightest clue—the flicker of an eyelid, the intake of breath—to warn him of his adversary's next move: feint or final strike. The killer gave no hint which direction he would attack from. His black eyes transfixed Bolan with a soulless, impersonal hatred that might have unnerved a lesser man. It was as if the guy had looked Death in the face and stared Death down.

The assailant was dressed from head to toe in a soft black combat suit. Both men wore the color of death.

Feeling surged back into Bolan's shoulder. He brought the wooden pole across in another vicious arc. His opponent sprang back.

Both of them were twisting around to renew the assault, each seeking the best position for attack.

The man's smooth Oriental features were marred with a puckered scar that pulled the corner of his mouth into a superior sneer. Bolan watched as his right hand reached back and emerged with a throwing knife. They were too close for it to be used for its proper purpose: instead, the killer came in low, lunging for the big man's ribs.

Bolan sidestepped, half turning as he slashed the extended knife hand and punched the heel of his own right hand under the assassin's chin. Seizing the initiative, Bolan shifted to grasp the wrist of his unbalanced opponent and began to twist outward.

The knife dropped to the floor. Bolan kicked it away.

But damage had been done. The strength had been drained from Bolan's arm. Before he could complete

the brutal wrist wrench, the killer had given in to the
flow of Bolan's counterattack and made a chop at
the back of the tall man's knee.

Bolan went down.

The assailant got him from behind, fingers of steel
probing for the vital pressure point.

A molten ball of pain exploded in Bolan's head.

At that moment the big guy knew who had killed
the computer genius and precisely how he had died.
He, too, was experiencing the searing agony that
Shinoda had suffered in his final moments. A sudden *ninja*-style leap of that Alvarez Street wall, and
then. . . .

A massive pounding reverberated in his ears.

A tortured howling echoed in his skull. It might
have been a siren. It might have been the roar that
ripped from his throat as he fell into a bottomless pit
of darkness.

Utter darkness.

"HE WASN'T THERE. . . ."

Those were the first words Bolan forced from his
parched throat. April Rose looked across at Hal
Brognola as she exhaled a sigh of relief.

Three faces slowly swam into focus. Darker,
hovering ovals within the shimmering shadows of
returning consciousness. . .features. . .then, finally,
familiar faces: April Rose grinning bravely; Hal
Brognola, with a cold cigar clamped between his
teeth, and Dr. Vicky Stevens.

"He wasn't there," Bolan repeated groggily as he
struggled to prop himself up on one elbow.

"I *said* you should have waited for the X-ray
results," Dr. Stevens chided him. She was putting the

best face on things, but her seemingly flippant reaction did not disguise the iron in her voice.

Bolan massaged his neck. He was back in the medical center. He sat up. "You must have got there—"

"Just in time," confirmed the man from Washington. Brognola, the liaison officer between the highest reaches of government and the man who headed the Stony Man team, was only too aware that Bolan was involved in this Shinoda problem on his direct orders. "Garfield had just found you when I got there. You were out for the count."

"But you grabbed. . . ."

"No," Brognola shook his head abruptly. "There was no sign of him."

Brognola was about to give a fuller explanation but checked himself and glared at Dr. Stevens as if she were an unwelcome visitor in her own clinic.

Nerves were understandably frayed, she decided, but before leaving she touched Bolan on the arm. "This time you don't go anywhere until I check you out. Personally."

Her concern was sincere. In every way.

"Okay, doctor, you've got it," Bolan promised her with a slight smile.

April Rose clenched her jaw, signaling that she alone would insure her guy regained his peak of health.

Vicky Stevens turned for the door but not before firing a final glance at Brognola that warned him it was more than his life was worth to light that cigar.

The Washington executive raised his eyebrows when she had left. "Tough lady!"

"We've all got our jobs to do," Bolan said.

"Yep, you're right," he nodded. "As I was saying,

Striker, by the time we'd checked you out and then figured he must have swung down to the balcony beneath—well, he was gone."

"And he'd taken the pictures with him. . . ."

Brognola nodded. "He scared the hell out of the lady who lives in the apartment under Shinoda's. She'd just got up to go to the bathroom when he came charging through. Still, we've got a description."

"I know who it was," Bolan stated simply. "It was Zeko Tanaga."

"I thought he was dead," grunted Brognola. But he did not question Bolan's identification. Striker's powers of recognition had been amply demonstrated in the past; his eidetic memory had put face to name with invariable accuracy.

"There'll be no need to look for him," said Bolan. "At least, not around here. He'll be out of the country by now—that was his specialty."

"Yeah. Borders didn't exist for him," nodded Brognola. "He could smuggle arms, men, explosives—whatever was needed to cause trouble—into any country he wanted. And then get out again."

"He was the advance man in Israel for the Red Army attack on the civilians at Lod Airport," Bolan said.

"That's right. And he was the only one that got away."

"As soon as I get to a secure phone, I'll call the Farm for an update," said April Rose, "but I'm sure the last we heard of Tanaga was that he'd been killed by a land mine at a terrorist recruiting camp in Yemen."

"Sounds like a useful cover story—I don't suppose

it was ever independently substantiated," Bolan said, his sardonic grin more teeth than humor. He rubbed his neck again. "I can vouch that Zeko Tanaga is very much alive."

They were silent for a moment, each trying to digest the implications of Tanaga's involvement.

Bolan was still puzzled how he had been taken unawares. That sixth sense, which had so often saved his life in the past, had issued no warning; the instinctual sonar with which the Executioner continuously swept his surroundings had not picked up the slightest hint of Tanaga's approach. It was as if he had not been there. . .and it baffled Bolan.

From Interpol files, CIA profiles, SAS reports, Mack Bolan knew the biographical outline of the shadowy terrorist who was probably wanted by more security agencies than The Jackal, but this was the first time their paths had crossed—and Bolan knew it would not be the last. He sensed that his close brush with death was only the prelude to a bloodier, more terrible conflict.

"We'd better get you out of here," said Brognola, shifting the unlighted cigar to the other side of his mouth. "I've borrowed the office from Jim Garfield. Kurtzman is waiting to give us a rundown on the technical angle."

"I'll get Dr. Stevens," said April Rose.

Bolan watched her walk to the door.

They were alone and Brognola's next words only served to underscore the big man's sense of foreboding.

"This Shinoda thing—to the city cops and even to agents like Garfield, well, it's just another killing. But I have a bad feeling it's going to take on a much greater importance—'' Brognola paused, searching for an appropriate parallel "—like Hitler's fake attack on that Polish radio station.... This could be the opening shot that will plunge the world into war. And I mean the whole world. Nobody will escape this time around.''

5

BROGNOLA FLICKED his lighter once, twice. It didn't work. He searched through the accumulated paperwork on Garfield's desk for a book of matches.

The federal agent's office had been pressed into service as a temporary command center for the team from Stony Man Farm, the Executioner's headquarters in Virginia's peaceful Shenandoah Valley, from which was waged a relentless war against the forces of terror, the blind armies of destruction and chaos.

Normally, in L.A., they would have used Able Team's aid, but Gadgets, Pol and Carl were on their way from a major clash in Cairo to an explosive mission in Azatlan, Mexico.

The three top Stony people now awaited Kurtzman before beginning the briefing.

April Rose stood by the window watching the patterns formed by the unseasonable rain. The silvery light that pierced the slate gray clouds gave her naturally lustrous hair an especially delicate sheen.

Bolan was standing slightly to one side. She really was a most striking woman. "Yes, I do," he said.

Her beautiful brows arched in bemusement.

"I like what I see, April," explained Bolan.

She chuckled lightly, remembering the first thing she had ever said to him. In defense against Bolan's surprise at finding her assigned to drive his War

Wagon, she had challenged him with, "You don't like what you see?" He did, of course; and over the many months of working together he had come to appreciate her unique blend of beauty and brains, for April Rose was every bit as smart as she was beautiful.

"Are you feeling up to this?" she said.

He nodded, then managed a tight grin to help banish her fears.

She had seen Bolan face danger before, but he had never looked so tired, and—she was almost afraid to admit it—so shaken as he had in that room at the clinic. He must be very concerned at how he had fallen victim to the recent attack, as if he had come across a new kind of warfare unknown in the city streets of America, let alone in the badlands of Nicaragua, or the hills of Tuscany.

Kurtzman came in carrying a tray with four full mugs and a large brown envelope tucked under his arm. "Found the makings for coffee in the lab. Thought we could all do with one."

Aaron Kurtzman—The Bear, as he was known—was Stony Man's resident computer expert. He had been checking through Shinoda's latest project material to round out the profile that had been prepared by April Rose.

April picked up two of the mugs and handed one across to Bolan. "Here, Striker. Hope it's strong enough for you."

Brognola drew at his cigar, then tipped his head at April, signaling it was time to begin.

She flipped open the file and glanced at her notes for a moment. "Kenji Shinoda was thirty-seven. His family had been here for two generations; they were honest and hardworking. His father had served bravely with a special nisei detachment in the Pacific."

"That's a part of the war too few people know about," noted Brognola. "Most of the writers today concentrate on the Japanese-Americans who were interned. But a lot of them fought for the Stars and Stripes."

"Shinoda's father was decorated for valor at Iwo Jima," continued April Rose. "And his uncle was a top cryptanalyst—he decoded ultrasecret communications from the Japanese High Command."

"Seems to have run in the family," observed Bolan.

"Kenji was bright at school. He got the highest grades from the start. He was a real achiever—maybe an overachiever. Specialized in math and computing at college. He won a postdoctoral fellowship at M.I.T., then came back to the West Coast to work in a think tank up in the Silicon Valley. Since then he'd headed several projects for both government and private industry."

"Sounds like a workaholic," grunted Brognola, scarcely the man to level such a criticism. "He couldn't have had much time for play."

"The opposite was true," corrected April Rose. "He was into martial arts, photography, and he liked to travel. His most recent trip was to Japan to visit the Shinodas' ancestral home—it's on the coast of a small peninsula south of Tokyo."

"Yeah, I saw his holiday snaps," muttered Mack Bolan.

"He was also an excellent chess player. He once advanced to the Pan-American finals but was beaten by Luis Domingo, who used the tricky Von Steinberg sacrifice. I'm afraid it was a bad year for Shinoda. He was also up for an American Science Award but he lost that to.... Let's see, a chemist...."

She ran her fingertip down the sheet to check the name. Kurtzman, who had been busy filling his pipe, looked up. "Okawa. And he's a biochemist."

"Right. Akira Okawa, another Japanese-American. Apparently the friction between them has continued for some time. Shinoda tried to get Okawa to work with him, but Okawa declined. Anyway, from what I can gather, if most of Shinoda's work hadn't been so secret he would probably have been nominated for a Nobel Prize."

"That's for sure," Kurtzman concurred. He turned over the envelope on which he had made a series of notes. "I've been going through some of his papers. There's no question that the man was a genius. He was working on something quite revolutionary, and he was years ahead of anyone else in the field. He was brilliantly inventive when it came to codes and ciphers. His latest success is the Checkmate program."

Kurtzman looked around to make sure that recognition registered in his listeners.

"The problem in recent years was that the techniques Shinoda devised were outstripping the capabilities of the machines available, so he turned to developing a new generation of computers. No, that's misleading—to use the word 'generation' suggests they'd merely be an improvement on the existing models. Shinoda was designing a whole new species of computer—one that would have organic or, in a sense, *living* components."

"Sounds like science-fiction," said Bolan.

"It's science-reality, I assure you." Kurtzman looked at the jottings he had made and shook his head in private admiration, the kind of respect that only one expert could have for another.

"The first modern large-scale electronic digital computer—ENIAC—had more than thirty tons of hardware, including eighteen thousand vacuum tubes," he explained. "The development of transistors meant a huge improvement, but the major breakthrough came with the silicon chip. As the hardware got smaller it was still able to handle increasingly more complex software."

"But this wasn't enough for Shinoda?" prompted Brognola.

"Exactly. He abandoned further miniaturization in order to work directly on the molecular level. Shinoda was completing the blueprint needed to utilize crystal lattices and bacteria as the heart of a new computer system."

"So the bugs would be back in the computer," joked April Rose.

"You could say that," smiled Kurtzman. "Controlled bacteria would provide the switching process within these protein-based biochips. This strange mix of genetic engineering and electronics could produce a machine that could calculate at perhaps a million times the speed of the fastest equipment available today, and it would have maybe ten million times the memory capacity."

"Too much," April heard herself saying.

"Truly awesome," agreed Kurtzman. "These new machines could handle coded communications of a complexity undreamed of—except by a man like Kenji Shinoda.''

"Computers like that could do a lot of other things, too,'' said Bolan.

"And that's what we've got to worry about,'' said Brognola. "The implications are extraordinary and terrifying.''

"Think what it would mean to the space race,'' said April Rose, doodling on the cover of her file. "Whoever developed this organic component, this biochip, will be able to leap years ahead.''

"Don't forget weapons' development and the coordination of defense systems,'' added Kurtzman. "In the areas of storage, retrieval and processing of intelligence data, it would make the present systems obsolete.''

Bolan had the picture. He did not need any more of the colors filled in. Now he knew with chilling clarity that Brognola had not been exaggerating when he had likened Shinoda's murder to the Nazi shots that sparked World War II. The nation that controlled the new computers would be assured of a military and technological edge for many years, perhaps decades, to come.

The man from Washington put Bolan's thoughts to words when he said: "For my money, this thing's got nothing to do with the codes specifically but everything to do with this new computer idea.''

Each of the experts in counterterror nodded in agreement.

Bolan glanced across at Kurtzman and the strikingly beautiful woman who were such an essential part of the Stony Man team. "I think you two should concentrate on the computer angle—you both have the qualifications. Find out just how far he'd gotten, who he'd worked on it with and if he had any real rivals in the field.''

"Quite a few papers will have to be cleared," warned Kurtzman.

"It'll be done. You can count on it," Brognola cut in. He then turned to look at Bolan. "And you, Mack, you've got to find out what a 'dead' terrorist has to do with organic computer science. We've got to know who the hell Zeko Tanaga is working for— there's obviously been nothing on him since he was reported blown away in Yemen."

April Rose flipped to another page in her notes. "Even before the KGB recruited him as an instructor, the Japanese Red Army had disowned him—he was too violent for them."

No one smiled at her understatement.

"I'll need some hours to rig a good cover for you, Striker. After that you're on your own," said Brognola.

Bolan nodded.

He knew exactly where he was going to start.

6

THEY CAME AT HIM from the front: two big men angling in from left and right. Bolan took on the black giant in the white combat suit first. As an ebony hand lunged forward, fingers opening for a face claw, Bolan weaved sideways and parried the intended strike.

Karl Brandt, standing at the edge of the mat, folded his arms in satisfaction, admiring the way their visitor had quickly shifted his ground so that the first attacker's body effectively blocked the second man from launching his own assault. In fact, the other guy never got the chance. Bolan applied the necessary leverage to propel the black man backward into his partner.

"Great!" Brandt clapped his hands once. The bout was over. Bolan's two opponents each gave him a short, respectful bow. He exchanged the courtesy before walking away with Karl Brandt, the owner and organizer of the Iron Fist Association. There was a confident spring in his step.

"Excellent, Colonel Phoenix. You have an interesting technique. Unorthodox, but effective."

"It works."

"That's what counts."

Bolan had arrived during an expert-level sparring practice. He had accepted the friendly challenge to join in as a useful prelude to questioning the martial arts instructor about Kenji Shinoda.

He had acquitted himself well.

Brandt was willing to talk to him.

"Let's go to my office. But I don't know if I can tell you anything that'll help."

The office was impressive. Neo-barbarian with lots of leather, metal, dark polished wood. Since returning from Nam, ex-Green Beret Brandt had enjoyed considerable success by capitalizing on the popularity of combat sports following the fad for kung fu movies. Actually he had made most of his money from the expanding chain of Tomorrow's Woman fitness centers, but his first love remained the private karate sessions with a circle of select students.

Bolan recognized Brandt as the sparring partner who had been featured in the photographs found on the floor of Shinoda's apartment.

"How good was he?"

"Shinoda? He was good—technically, that is. Very competitive. Perhaps too much so," Brandt told him. "Ken could think fast on his feet, but he could never get beyond that."

"What do you mean?"

"He never emptied out his mind. He never trusted that the movements would flow from pure instinct." Brandt appreciated that the big man on the other side of his desk could grasp very clearly what he was trying to say. "To achieve the maximum physical effect, the intellect must be stilled, bypassed even. Ken Shinoda was always thinking about something, even on the practice mat...thinking about his work, money, women, maybe just the next stance, the next throw."

The phone rang.

"Excuse me."

It was Brandt's lawyer. They discussed a legal complexity concerning the latest franchise for a Tomorrow's Woman spa that someone wanted to open in Boulder, Colorado.

With his smoothly tanned shaven head and square, toughened hands, Karl Brandt looked out of place in his West Los Angeles business office. He dug into the informal clutter of promotional material to find the contract the lawyer was talking about. Give him a gold earring and some black leather, thought Bolan, and he could have passed for one of those killer bikers on Catalina that Carl Lyons and his Able Team colleagues had blown away in the nick of time. But there was a lively intelligence in Brandt's eyes that said he was too smart to turn the deadly skills he had learned in a faraway combat zone into psychopathic behavior.

They were arguing over clause 23(d). It gave Bolan a chance to look around the office. The counter of the long, low side-cabinet was crammed with competition trophies, souvenirs of Nam, a vegetable-juice blender, the model of a very beautiful yacht and some framed photos.

Bolan recognized two of the pictures. One showed Brandt working out with Richard Gere. The actor had signed it with a personal message for Karl. The other photo was of a bout with Shinoda.

Brandt put the phone down.

"When did you last see him?" Bolan asked, nodding toward the photo.

"About three weeks ago. I'd been expecting to hear from him, then you turned up with the news.

He'd just got back from Japan. The holiday had done him good—he seemed to be on top of the world.''

"Why were you expecting to hear from him?''

"Oh, he'd finally decided to buy the *Diana*.'' Brandt tipped his head toward the model of the magnificent ketch-rigged motor sailer. "First he wanted her, then he didn't, but when he came back from Japan he said he wanted to buy her for sure.''

"Could I ask how much a boat like that would cost?''

The phone rang again.

Brandt picked it up but cupped his hand over the mouthpiece as he replied to Bolan's inquiry, "I wouldn't give you much change out of a quarter of a million.''

It was obvious that such a large and luxurious boat could bring in big money on the open market, but this asking price was steeper than Bolan had expected. Karl Brandt was doing all right for himself. And Shinoda had apparently found some way to come up with that kind of bread. Bolan assumed it did not involve a loan from the local bank.

Maybe there was a lot more to this than simple blackmail.

Maybe Shinoda was going to market his plans for the bio-organic computer device to the highest bidder.

If indeed he had been prepared to sell out his country, then Kenji Shinoda had paid in full for his intended treachery. But Bolan had a sour taste in his mouth nevertheless.

And it was imperative to find out who the computer genius was dealing with.

"Yeah, after you've paid the membership fee, you can pay for specialized tuition on a monthly basis." This routine call should have been handled in the reception area but, although he raised his eyebrows to signal an apology for the interruption, Brandt did not seem to mind dealing with it—after all, business was business. "So you're interested in the *ninja* program. Let me check when the next series of classes is due to start."

Brandt pushed the contract he had previously dealt with to one side and slid out one of the promotional brochures.

Bolan, who looked at the folder from the far side of the desk, was startled to see the cover shot of a man in an all-black combat outfit. It might have been himself in action.

Not realizing his guest's attention was focused on the publicity photo, Brandt flipped open the booklet. "We've got a new group starting in two weeks. It'll be taught by Don Kalamoko. He's very good. It's not for beginners, you know.... I see, two years of *tae kwon-do*.... That's good, hope we'll see you then. Goodbye."

"What is that?" Bolan's eyes indicated the brochure.

"Oh, it's a gimmick, really," confessed Brandt. "First they all wanted to be the new Bruce Lee... then they wanted to be the next Chuck Norris.... Now all the hotshots want to get *ninja* training. Well, we try to give them what they want!"

"Give me your opinion of the *ninja*."

"They're probably the most feared martial artists in the world," Brandt said. "And the most secretive, as I'm sure you know. They started out in feudal times as the trusted messengers and bodyguards of the Japanese warlords, but gradually they evolved into spies and assassins. Their special skills, or *ninjutsu*, are the arts of stealth and invisibility.''

Brandt shifted the papers on the desk again and revealed a wooden filing tray. He fished out a metal throwing star and slid it across the desk for Bolan to inspect.

''Nasty little thing, isn't it? You've seen it—it's called a *shaken*. It's razor sharp, so watch your fingers. And that's just one item from their bag of tricks. The *ninja* can use anything from blowpipes to a bizarre sickle-and-chain weapon called a *kusar-igama*. If they get close enough, which they can do with ease, the *ninja* can kill a man with one finger.''

Bolan could vouch for that, as could his Phoenix Force, recent victors over the most extreme *ninja* forces—but The Executioner chose to say nothing.

''Many of the *ninja* are trained from childhood, the secrets passed down from father to son. They are taught running, swimming and climbing from the time they are infants. It requires fantastic discipline. That's why I called our program something of a gimmick. We in the West don't know half their tricks and methods, and even if we did, can you imagine teaching some overweight stockbroker how to scale a smooth wall using a *ninja*'s cat's claws? No, they just want to impress their buddies or their girl friends, so we play along.''

Bolan nodded with a smile. At least Brandt was honest with himself. But Bolan had recently crossed paths with a man who could kill with one hand and then escape down a high wall. And he had to find him.

The instructor might as well have been reading his mind, for the next thing Brandt said was, "If anyone really wants to learn the secrets of the *ninja*, they have to go to Japan."

7

BOLAN HOPED Kingoro Nakada would be there to meet the plane. The newly appointed head of Japanese security would be able to clear him through customs and immigration via the back door, just as Hal Brognola had attended to such matters in Los Angeles. Otherwise there might be some awkward questions about what was in Bolan's briefcase. He had chosen to bring overseas only one weapon—the Beretta 93-R, distant cousin of his original Brigadier "Belle," an automatic tooled for the kind of action Mack Bolan, a.k.a. John Phoenix, could expect to run into anywhere in the world.

His cover was simple. It had been worked out by the head Fed from Washington Wonderland.

John Phoenix, a "retired officer and advisor on high-level selected security arrangements for both federal and selected local agencies," was on a roving commission prior to submitting a report "for updating the organization and the effectiveness of certain security details." His suggestions might affect a lot of units—from the LAPD to the President's own bodyguard.

Commander Nakada, whose own background seemed to parallel the one contrived for Colonel Phoenix—at least the version given to him during the long-distance call from Brognola—was happy to play host to such an expert visitor. They would have a lot to talk about, and he looked forward to a frank and useful exchange.

That was just what Brognola wanted Nakada to think. Although Bolan was operating a long way from home base and without any of the customary support systems of Stony Man Farm, the cover plan gave him a some immunity, freedom of movement, and invaluable contacts.

The No Smoking sign went out and Bolan reached for the crumpled pack in his shirt pocket. Suzy Kenton, a stewardess, watched him light up and take a deep drag before she turned away to check on the coffee that was brewing; she would like to offer this man something stronger, but a sixth sense told her the big guy would take coffee, black.

Bolan brooded on what he knew about the *ninja*, as art and as menace. The five fine Stony men of Phoenix Force had experienced a bloody confrontation with *ninja* terrorists when a misguided attempt to "avenge" Hiroshima and Nagasaki had imperiled countless millions of Americans innocent of any antagonism whatsoever toward their Japanese allies.

Phoenix Force had reported to him of the war tools and techniques they had so bravely and unflinchingly come up against, and it was one hell of a story. Bolan had been absorbed by their accounts of the *ninja*'s use of the short sword, and horsehair garrotes, and the many ruses they had devised to conceal themselves for the final strike. From his own studies, Bolan knew that if ever a *ninja* was cornered, he would bite off his own tongue rather than talk. Bolan was both repelled and fascinated by the *ninja*.

One thing struck the Executioner as bizarre: the

contrast between the dedication and discipline needed to master the *ninja*'s arts, however misguided, and Zeko Tanaga's supposedly ungovernable temper. As far as Bolan could see, the strength of the *ninja* lay in their absolutely iron-willed control, not in outbursts of unpredictable violence. In the full bloom of his bloody career, something—or someone—had changed Tanaga.

The memory of those soulless eyes still haunted Bolan. And he was certain the answer to the puzzle lay in the *ninja*'s homeland, just as surely as the other keys to the Shinoda mystery awaited him there.

The stewardess approached with refreshments. She served the balding owner of a Tokyo franchise, found an extra pillow for his wife, then she reached Bolan's seat.

"Would you care for something from the bar, sir?" Suzy stared straight down into those steely blue eyes.

"Coffee will be fine. Black, please."

The stewardess smiled to herself as she poured a full measure of the strong brew into a plastic cup. Suzy knew who she was going to bed with tonight— at least in her dreams.

Her hand brushed against his, sending a tingle up her spine as she handed him a couple of the latest magazines and a pamphlet. There was an aura of excitement that surrounded this Colonel Phoenix—she had checked his name on the passenger manifest— and Suzy found it extremely enticing.

Bolan watched as the honey blonde in the trimly fitting uniform walked back down the aisle, then began flipping through the publicity brochure she had given him.

The tourist booklet was called *Japan: Land of Happy Contrasts*. The picture of an ageless sampan sailing up the Inland Sea was contrasted with a photo of the sleek "bullet" locomotive, one of the world's fastest passenger trains. A photograph of the neon-lit streets of Tokyo, brighter even than those of Las Vegas, was set alongside a delicate composition emphasizing the mossy quiet of a Zen garden. And blue-robed kendo students were pictured opposite some hot-dog skiers in the Japanese alps. The old and the new, the timeless and the latest fad—Japan had a foot in both worlds.

Bolan glanced at the picture of a little girl watching an aged craftsman creating an exquisite doll—the toddler looked like a little doll herself. How curious it was, he reflected, that a land of such beauty should also nurture the seeds of senseless terrorist violence.

The deep blue waters of the Pacific sparkled far below between the misty gaps in the clouds. Bolan wished he was going to Japan on a peaceful mission. Each time he crossed this ocean, he was going to war....

He picked up *Seven Days*, one of the weekly newsmagazines. The stewardess was coming back with ginger-ale mixer for the guy who owned the car dealership. Bolan looked up at her and was rewarded with a we-should-get-together-sometime smile. He gave her a smile as he turned back to the photo-news section and was confronted with a face like ones he had seen a thousand times before in newsmagazines and on the front pages of the daily papers. It was from Belfast.

The photo showed a young girl standing outside the ruined front of a neighborhood baker's shop—

her mother had just gone inside for a loaf when the bomb had exploded. The camera caught that look of utter fear mixed with blank incomprehension that Bolan had seen reflected in the faces of so many innocent victims of rabid terrorism.

Anger flared into a steady white-hot flame as Bolan twisted his head away. That poor Irish youngster did not know the difference between political theories and cared even less, but she had lost her mother in the name of some vicious ideological abstraction.

No, not abstraction.

These bastards wanted power. Pure and simple. And it was very real; it was not an abstraction. They did not care whom they murdered in their attempt to seize control.

Assassins trained by the KGB's Department V outside Moscow; explosives experts supplied through Libya; Bulgarian hit men; Red Armies and Red Columns and Red Brigades; the ordinary "soldiers" sucked in by the unending propaganda spewed out from the Kremlin's sewers. . . all these killed innocent bystanders, killed anyone who stood in their way— and all in the name of their perverted ideas.

But what they really wanted to establish was a new order in which they were to be forever above others less fortunate, an order that would give them the freedom to pillage at will. It was not simply a question of Bolan's private convictions, it was a matter of public record—the evidence of modern history.

Yeah, Bolan knew these killers. He knew them well. Their ruthless business depended on the fact that no one in authority would stand up to them. Spineless politicians gave terrorists the freedom to wage their bloody campaigns against innocent targets.

Well, Mack Bolan was a death-dealer too, when he had to be.

There are times in the history of all civilized societies when the gap between the law and simple justice becomes stretched to the breaking point; when the machinery for protecting decent hardworking folk spins its wheels on the fine points of intricate legal niceties, while the common man's sense of justice is outraged. These are the times that call for a special man to redress the balance.

In British legend, when Prince John misruled during the absence of his brother, Richard Coeur de Lion, the people's cause was championed by an outlaw who lived in the deepest forest: Robin Hood.

In the American West, even if the storytellers do garnish reality, men like Bat Masterson and the Earp brothers used their guns to force murderous desperadoes to toe the line.

In other eras, in other places, citizens' rights have been defended by an outlaw hero.

Today, times call for an executioner.

The Executioner.

Bolan had served two tours in Nam, then spent the intervening years waging his private war against the Mafia. Now he and the small but mighty team of handpicked warriors that backed him were facing a new enemy.

Bolan was striking back.

He was fighting for that bewildered kid on a Belfast street. He was putting his life on the line to protect a teacher or a farmer's family in some far-off land, to insure that yet another area of the map was not to be colored in a Russian shade of red. And, as always, he was willing to risk everything for the country he loved and believed in.

Bolan knew with utter certainty why this new war was so important, why it had to be fought—alone, if necessary.

FIVE FACES.

That's all he had to go on, really. The hulking guy with half his little finger missing; the older fellow with the white streak in his hair; the studious one with the spectacles, possibly just a visitor; the woman, pretty in an unmemorable sort of way, and finally the terrorist, long since presumed dead.

It was going to be like looking for a goddamned needle in a haystack.

The airport facilities were jammed with passengers from three incoming flights. Other people thronged the arrivals area, jostling to catch a glimpse of a longed-for visitor or returning relative. Outside, there were more than a hundred million inhabitants crowded onto an island chain that was not as big as California.

It seemed an impossible task.

Bolan, standing taller than most, scanned the crush for any sign of someone sent to meet him.

A young American woman was being questioned about her visa dates.

"Oh, for Pete's sake, this is the third time I've visited your country in the last year—of course my passport is in order."

The Japanese officer looked at her but remained expressionless. He waited for a colleague to come over and gang up with him.

Poor kid, thought Bolan, *what a way to start a trip.* She had longish hair pulled back in a rather severe bun, horn-rimmed glasses that only magnified the puzzled expression in her eyes and a wide mouth now set in a defiantly compressed line.

The second official walked over, and she repeated herself in passably fluent Japanese. The two men were clearly surprised at this but gave no indication of having understood her.

The woman tried a third time, reverting to English, and now they caught her meaning. Apparently the Japanese can handle English, but they are not at ease with a foreigner who can talk back to them in their own language.

A guy in a blue raincoat recognized Bolan from prior intel and gave a brief wave to attract his attention. The big American followed him through a door at the side of the reception area. He left wondering how the woman would make out.

In the quiet of the corridor on the far side of the door they introduced themselves.

"Kingoro Nakada. Call me King," said the guy in the raincoat. "It is my nickname, I'm afraid. Sorry I was late—a traffic accident snarled things up."

The only person they passed using this detour around the bureaucratic barrier was an old janitor pushing a metal bin of cleaning supplies. Might be a useful way to sneak through this airport's security, Bolan noted, not out of any malicious intent but simply because he always filed such information.

Nakada's car was waiting outside in a No Stopping zone. It was a dark Toyota limousine. The woman behind the wheel got out and opened the rear door for them.

"This is Setsuko Seki, my driver—I call her Suki. She worked with me for a while on homicide. I brought her along when I was transferred a month ago."

"Hello, Suki."

She returned Bolan's casual smile. Although in plain clothes—a green skirt and lighter, pastel blouse—she wore them neatly, very like a uniform.

Suki was undoubtedly an expert driver. Anyone who could maneuver through the Tokyo rush hour would have no problem in the qualifying heats for Formula One racing.

Staring out the window, Bolan realized just how green so many American cities were, even in their busy downtown sections; here, few parks or trees relieved the relentlessly dynamic sprawl of the Japanese capital. The noisy core of the city was ringed with crisscrossed layers of expressways, each feeding more cars into the swirling flood of traffic.

"Hang on," Suki said calmly, as she roared ahead of a taxi to be first through a narrowed roadway caused by the jackhammer confusion of a new construction project. The taxi driver blared out a protest at being so unexpectedly cut off.

"Not all our young kamikaze pilots sacrificed themselves in the war, you know," remarked Nakada, nodding toward the rear window. "Some of them went on to become taxi drivers. But they don't like Clause Nine, of course."

Bolan looked across at his host, who seemed to be enjoying the joke he must have told to a dozen different visitors.

"In our 1948 Constitution, in Clause Nine, the Japanese people renounced war forever. But those guys out there want their old jobs back—they say it was a lot safer!"

Bolan managed a polite grin. In his mind he was constantly reviewing the few slim leads he had to work on. But he would have to keep playing the wide-eyed tourist if he was to discover the scenery he had memorized from Shinoda's pictures.

Kingoro Nakada was explaining the local setup. "Having decided to have no more to do with war, Japan has no need for an offensive military machine and therefore no military secrets. And so, officially, we have no intelligence service as such. My unit is recruited from various police departments and the Self-Defense Forces—I've served in both. Security for visiting VIPs and for some of our own leaders is our mandate, but this involves a certain amount of intelligence work to keep tabs on known trouble-makers."

"I'd be very interested to see your procedures in that area. We might be able to exchange some useful suggestions," Bolan said, mindful of the newcomer's role he was playing.

"Good. I've arranged for you to be given a guided tour tomorrow morning. But first I'd like to show you my city. If you're not the victim of jet lag I'd be honored to take you to dinner this evening."

Bolan nodded his acceptance.

Kingoro Nakada leaned forward. "Would you pick Colonel Phoenix up at eight, please, Suki?"

8

THE HOTEL might have been situated anywhere; it was a massive maze of corridors, punctuated only by identical doors spaced at identical intervals.

In the bathroom Bolan found a toothbrush and a disposable razor wrapped in cellophane. Everything was safely sanitized. If it were not for the small pamphlet on Buddhist scriptures lying next to the Bible, and the tiredness he felt from the long flight, Bolan could have been in Minneapolis.

He flipped on the television as he unpacked his suitcase. The big event seemed to be a grotesquely phony midget wrestling match. He punched the Off switch and flaked out on the bed.

Suki was precisely on schedule. She called up to his room, and Bolan was ready.

"Commander Nakada presents his apologies," Suki explained as Bolan got into the car. This time he rode up front with her. "He's still tied up at the office but he'll meet us at the restaurant."

Suki had obviously had time to go home and change. She was now wearing a wraparound skirt and embroidered silk top with loose sleeves. While the outfit was thoroughly modern, it held more than a graceful suggestion of the traditional kimono. Her hair, sleek and black as a raven's wing, was piled back and pinned in an artfully casual manner.

Tokyo by night was even noisier than Tokyo by day. Vendors' cries, bicycle bells, the unending bustle of street business were interwoven with the roar of traffic. Overhead a dazzling display of neon signs screamed out their incomprehensible messages.

"Although he's officially resigned from Homicide, the commander still makes himself available to help clear up some of the outstanding cases," Suki said, amplifying her original apology. Her eyes, framed with soft, sooty lashes, swept the scene. "He's known as King of the City. It was a hard-won title and not one he'll give up easily."

"How about you?" asked Bolan. "Are you happy to have been transferred?"

"It is difficult," she replied, "so much more difficult for a woman to get ahead in Japan than it must be in America. I would have been foolish to refuse the opportunity of this new position."

They stopped at a pedestrian crosswalk. The car window was open. Bolan inhaled the curious blend of incense and rotting fish, of Hilite cigarettes, of fresh-cut flowers and boiling rice, and the sheer press of humanity—that indefinable but distinctive aroma of the Orient.

Bolan's attention focused on the side mirror. He adjusted it to inspect the car now third back from them. It was not possible to make out any details, but it appeared to have a number of men in it. Bolan felt sure he had seen it back at the hotel, just a detail picked up at the periphery of watchfulness. Probably innocent businessmen on their way to a sumo match....

"Some of the things I saw—well, perhaps this job is better, because one never gets used to the sight of death, Colonel Phoenix.'' Suki glanced across at him sympathetically, as if thankful that their visitor would not have to inure himself to the gruesome consequences of random violence.

"I suppose not," said Bolan, who knew full well what she meant. He had lived with it longer than she had. He had learned to accept its necessity, its occasional justifiability, its inevitability—but get used to it, never.

"There he is," she said.

Bolan noticed for the first time just how big the policeman was; not as tall as himself maybe, but far bulkier and more broad-shouldered than the people around him. Nakada was standing on the edge of the sidewalk outside Miyasaki's restaurant, his presence defying anyone to fill the empty parking space in front of him.

He held a cigarette pinched between his teeth as he surveyed the scene with a proprietary interest. Nakada tossed the butt in the gutter as Suki slid the car over to the curb.

It was raining as Bolan got out. The large, warm drops had sparked a flurry of opening umbrellas. Bolan turned to check the traffic but the car that had aroused his curiosity had vanished.

Nakada steered his guest into the dimly lit restaurant, said hello to the owner and arranged that they should first inspect the kitchens at the rear. One of the cooks gave the commander a friendly nod. Nakada seemed quite at home here.

The cook picked up a razor-edged knife and demonstrated the slicing technique used to produce paper-thin shavings of raw fish.

Bolan noticed two senior chefs nearby closely observing one of their apprentices fillet a rather non-descript fish.

"Ah, he's learning how to prepare *fugu*," Nakada was delighted to explain. "One must earn a license to serve *fugu*. Certain organs in the blowfish contain a deadly poison and so they must be expertly removed before the fish can be cut up for sashimi or a seafood stew."

"One slip of the knife, one toxic part missed," added Suki, "and dinner would become as fatal as, what do you call it, 'Russian roulette.' "

"In that case, I think I'll stick to the beef," remarked Bolan.

"An excellent choice, sir," said Mr. Miyasaki. He had arrived in the kitchens to tell them that everything was ready.

Paper-latticed partitions were drawn back to reveal an intimate dining room. Only three places were laid around the low table. Nakada turned to Bolan. "I selected this place for its privacy. We may wish to talk over matters that we would not want any others to overhear. First we must remove our shoes."

Mr. Miyasaki fussed around, making sure they were comfortable.

"An advantage of police work, King, is the number of useful friends you can make," said Bolan as he seated himself on the floor by the ankle-high table.

"That's true," conceded Nakada, as the owner left with a deeply courteous bow, "but one also makes a lot of enemies."

"The Ikida case?" Suki asked him.

"No new developments," Nakada replied with a weary nod. "It's the affair I was helping out with this evening, Colonel Phoenix, a contract execution. But if we don't nail the killer soon, we might end up with a war on our hands.''

He watched Bolan handle his chopsticks with polished ease as the American deftly selected a morsel of pickled tomato. This *gaijin* was a man of mysterious depths, he thought to himself. And Nakada was surprised at his assessment, for he suspected that if Colonel Phoenix had not come with the highest recommendation, he might well have placed him on the far side of the law.

''Have you ever had to deal with industrial espionage?'' asked Bolan, making it sound as casually conversational as he could.

Nakada finished the last of the appetizer tidbits. ''No, that's not my field.... I cannot imagine it's as interesting as murder.''

The two men were psychologically circling each other like sumo wrestlers sizing each other up.

Suki, meanwhile, wanted to ask their visitor where he had learned to handle chopsticks so comfortably. Then she realized it was most likely that Colonel Phoenix had seen service in Vietnam, and she felt embarrassed at her earlier remarks in the car. ''I hope you will be here long enough to see some of the countryside outside Tokyo. Perhaps there will be time....''

Suddenly Bolan felt that prickling tingle. There was no mistaking the warning this time. He signaled with his hand like a television director that she should continue talking.

''...time for you to visit Mount Fuji or even Kyoto,'' Suki continued, playing along.

Nakada watched as Bolan slipped quietly to his

feet and moved with catlike grace across the golden matting. Bolan padded silently to the paper wall opposite the sliding partition through which they had entered.

Suki chattered on as Bolan reached for the latch.

Abruptly he slid the panel back, and the man outside tumbled into the room.

A second shadowy figure followed the first. He went straight for Bolan.

The other wall panel was yanked open, and two more hoods charged in.

"Watch out, King!" Bolan shouted the warning before grasping his attacker's wrist, using the man's own momentum to send him crashing into the first eavesdropper.

Nakada spun in one fluid movement to fend off the assault from his side. His right foot continued lifting in a high arc. The kick connected with the leading thug's rib cage, snapping bone as he was driven backward with a harsh yelp of pain.

Suki whirled around, pulling out the long pin in her hair. The two guys on the floor beside her were groggily sorting themselves out. The one with a pockmarked face was reaching into his jacket. She did not wait to find out what weapon was concealed in there; Suki stabbed him through the hand with the needle-sharp point.

A fifth goon appeared in the doorway, his goldcapped teeth flashing as he barked out an order for his men to retreat.

Bolan grabbed the nearest man before he could make a break. Using his hip as a lever, Bolan threw the punk onto the mat for a second time, following through with a smart chop to the neck. He wanted this guy in one piece—there were some questions he had to ask. The hardguy's partner, clutching at his punctured hand, took advantage of Bolan's momentary engagement to scuttle back to the corridor.

Nakada sent the last of the assailants flying with another kick to his fleeing rear. The thug stumbled forward and crashed through the flimsy paneling. Gold Teeth helped him to his feet, and they ran toward the kitchen exit.

The commander turned, saw the hoodlum at Bolan's feet sliding a knife from his pocket, and dropped with his knee smashing down across the windpipe. When Nakada got up, his target lay motionless, staring glassy-eyed across the floor at the spilled remains of the supper he had so unwisely disturbed.

The action could not have taken much more than sixty seconds—five against three in the confines of a private dining cubicle—but it looked as if great beasts had been on the rampage.

The splintered door frame hung on shreds of paper, and the dead man's foot rested in Bolan's sukiyaki.

Nakada turned to face the startled Mr. Miyasaki, who hovered between an apology that such a thing could have happened to his honored guests and shock at the sight of the damage. Suki calmly pushed the pin back in her hair, rearranging a fallen strand as if she had merely been caught in a gust of wind.

Bolan knelt to take a closer look at the corpse. He cursed under his breath that King's action had been so thorough, so terminal. Still, there had not been time to ask him to go easy. The knife was still clutched in the dead man's hand.

It riveted Bolan's attention. Not the knife, but the hand: the top two joints were missing from the little fingers, just like the big guy in the photograph.

9

"IT IS THE SIGN of the *yakuza*," said Nakada, slurring the word quickly so it sounded like "yuksa." "The mark of a gangster. As I told you, if a policeman in this city is honest, he will end up with some powerful enemies."

Bolan had had to ask twice before the security chief would give him a direct answer. The previous night, when they had escorted the American back to his hotel, both Nakada and Suki had almost tripped over each other with their profuse apologies. This morning Bolan wanted to know more about these mobsters of the Japanese *cosa nostra*.

They were driving south around the bay, well beyond the city limits, to Nakada's headquarters. The Japanese officer seemed preoccupied as he stared moodily out of the window.

"So the missing finger joint marks him as a soldier for the mob?" persisted Bolan.

"Yes. If a retainer should fail in a mission or somehow foul up, then he must cut off part of his finger with a samurai sword to atone for his mistakes—though it's so common a sight I suspect the *oyabun* sometimes set things up merely to test their lieutenants' loyalties."

"*Oyabun?*"

"They are what you would call the godfathers, but

they live more like *daimyo*, the great feudal lords of the past.''

''Tell me more about these *yakuza*.''

Nakada hesitated, searching for a place to start. ''Frankly, I don't know to what extent you've had to deal with gangsters in your own country, Colonel Phoenix, but I don't think the *yakuza* are quite the same as the Mafia.''

''Oh?''

''The *kumi*, the criminal clans and families, derive much of their income from the usual illegal sources—prostitution and pornography, drugs, gambling, blackmail, protection rackets. But they have as many legitimate fronts: hotels, nightclubs and discos, steakhouses, laundries and *pachinko*—you know, pinball—parlors. They can pass as pillars of the establishment. Indeed, they are often accepted as such. It's a seven-billion-dollar-a-year business.''

Mack Bolan felt a chill of recognition.

''Quite,'' nodded Suki. ''They also have close ties to several political groups and influential institutions, not to mention some of the *zaibatsu*, our giant corporations.''

''I think the point Suki is trying to make is that the *yakuza* are not to be trifled with, but they are a domestic problem and not likely to be of much interest to you, Colonel,'' Nakada said curtly, seemingly disturbed by his assistant's interruption. ''No, what we've got to worry about from the point of view of security are the international terrorist groups and the private armies. One of Japan's most famous novelists, Yukio Mishima, started his own private army. He committed hara-kiri when he saw it wasn't going anywhere. But there are others less romantic, more practical. Those are potentially the most dangerous. But the *yakuza* are not interested in causing trouble in our area. They don't want to draw that kind of attention to themselves.''

Bolan made no comment, but everything he had just learned about the *yakuza* make them sound sickeningly like the organization he had fought in the States.

"It'll take about another ten minutes to get there," the commander informed Bolan, relaxing slightly as he changed the subject. He tapped Suki lightly on the shoulder. "I'd like you to show Colonel Phoenix around the grounds and through our records department. Yamashita is expecting you. Then you can end the tour in my office."

They completed the journey in silence. As Bolan stared out at the market streets and warehouses and residential enclaves they passed, he tried to puzzle out the meaning behind the attack in the restaurant.

Was it some longstanding local hatred that had erupted? Were those thugs really out to get Nakada? If not, what interest could the *yakuza* have in Mack Bolan?

"Not at all like Virginia, is it, Colonel?"

Bolan looked across with a start.

Nakada controlled a small smile of satisfaction. After all that circling and probing, he had Phoenix pegged: he was certain now that the colonel was a colleague of Paul Ryan at the embassy. Nakada could not resist underlining this minor victory. "No, it's not at all like Langley."

Bolan gave the merest shake of his head. At first, he had thought Nakada was revealing some knowledge of the Stony Man operation. It was with relief that he realized Nakada was referring to the CIA.

Rather than being located in a modern concrete office block or in a more traditional Japanese villa, Nakada's headquarters were housed in a rambling Victorian monstrosity, complete with Gothic towers, decorative tiling, and a graveled driveway lined with chestnut trees. As their car approached the house, King Nakada described the place.

It had been built, in what was then almost a rural area, by Willem Reemeyer, a Dutch importer who had prospered during Yokohama's heyday as an international port. On a fateful morning—September 1, 1923—Willem and his wife, Mary, were seeing friends off at the docks. They both perished in the first massive shock wave of the Great Earthquake.

The house, so solid that it withstood the jolting tremor, was taken over in the reconstruction period as a storage center for the jumbled remnants of municipal records. Over the years it had passed through the hands of a dozen different governmental departments, finally being converted into the secluded HQ of the security team now headed by Nakada.

The huge riding stables had been altered to accommodate a gymnasium and firing range. The high walls had been strengthened and fitted with alarms.

Bolan could see a group of agents receiving training in hand-to-hand combat on the lawn, but they were lost from view as Suki drove up to the front steps.

"I'm sorry I must desert you," said Nakada, almost jumping from the car before it had stopped, "but I have many phone calls to make. I intend to get to the bottom of last night's unfortunate affair."

Bolan nodded pleasantly, thinking that was precisely what he, too, intended to do. "See you later then," he said.

It started raining again when Suki drove around the side of the mansion to leave the car in the garage where a small team of mechanics were making a thorough inspection of a heavyweight limo. Bolan guessed it was bulletproof and bomb-proof.

"Well, Suki," he said. "Let's go through Records first. There's a lot here I've got to see for myself."

MR. YAMASHITA had been on the staff longer than anyone else. Kingoro Nakada was the third boss he had had in the six and a half years since he had established the records department in the cavernous basement of the Reemeyer house. But in all that time, Colonel Phoenix was the first American to be shown through the guarded facilities.

Yamashita wore gold-rimmed glasses and only a light linen jacket, although the air conditioning kept his underground archives a little too cool for comfort. As he showed their visitor the computer connections that gave Nakada's unit access to the information filed by all sections of the Japanese National Police Agency, Bolan noticed that Yamashita would often punctuate his speech with a hiss. It was just a tactic to gain time to think over what he was about to say.

"Instead of describing how all this works, it would probably be easier to invent an example to demonstrate our system in action."

Yamashita paused again, and Bolan jumped at the chance to suggest, "Well, let's suppose you've had a tip-off concerning...oh, say, the United Red Army."

Yamashita hesitated yet again, but then he shrugged. One example was as good as another.

His sensitive fingers stroked over the keyboard as he alerted the machine of their request.

"Since Nagata and Sakaguchi were sentenced to death, the Red Army is pretty much a spent force," Suki said as they waited for the computer to print out its answer. "The group split apart. There was too much internal dissension."

The terminal chattered.

"I've asked for the printout in English," Yamashita told him. He seemed almost apologetic for having taken this initiative. "So much intelligence work is done in English."

The paper moved rapidly as the high-speed printer went to work. The first thing to emerge was a computerized diagram of the assumed power structure between known cells of the Red Army, with further references directing the user to individual files.

"That gives you the overview," said Yamashita, before Bolan could digest even a percentage of it, "and this is a listing of all known members by specialty."

The new sheet listed names under subheadings such as Explosives and Kidnapping. Again the reader was directed to separate files. Bolan scanned the lists of suspects. Tanaga's name was not there.

"Next it will produce a chronological digest of their activities. It takes some time—the machine is collecting information from various sources, including the Interpol link."

"Well, how about showing me some of these other files? How would you follow up on, er, *this* guy— Tanaka?" Bolan deliberately picked the closest name he could to the one that he sought.

"Like some coffee?" Suki asked.

Bolan nodded, and she went off to get some.

Yamashita unlocked the *T* drawer and opened it for Bolan's inspection. They were labeled in Japanese and English. The American pulled out Tanaka's folder. The guy had engineered a skyjacking in 1977.

The printing machine began to click excitedly. Yamashita walked back to check it.

Bolan quickly tugged up the Tanaga Zeko file and flipped it open. One look at the photo confirmed the identity; there was no mistaking that twisted sneer.

Presumed deceased, it said.

The information was the same as they had back in the States. And it had probably been fed into this network from the same tainted source.

So it was another dead end. In a way, not dead enough.

Both brown folders were back in place before Yamashita returned with another scroll of data on the Red Army.

Over coffee, Bolan asked, "What about these *yakuza*? What information do you have on—what was it King called them—the *oyabun*?"

Yamashita hissed twice before admitting, "Very little."

"The metropolitan police have the usual criminal records on the rank-and-file members of these gangs," added Suki, "but the *oyabun* themselves are respected as part of the establishment. They are looked up to as successful businessmen...." Her explanation tailed off into a frustrated shrug.

It was not until they were walking across the wet grass toward the gymnasium that Suki finished what she had to say. "You must understand, Colonel, that the top gangsters here have very influential connections with politicians... and with the police. Perhaps that is why there is so little information about them ever put on record."

SUKI WATCHED with increasing regard for the tall stranger as Bolan and his handpicked opponent bowed and took their positions. The tips of the bamboo swords clicked as they touched.

Benkei bared his teeth behind the metal face guard—he would cut this outsider down to size. He would show Yumoto, their tyrannical instructor, just how good he was.

"Hajima!" Yumoto gave the order to start, noting with some distaste how Benkei swaggered.

The trainee feinted, hoping to draw Bolan off balance. It did not work. He sliced in a downward chop. The visitor calmly parried the practice blade away.

Bolan stepped back quickly, and Benkei was tempted to follow with a quick jab to the breastplate. Again he was deflected.

Benkei tried for the head—he would rap this American on the left temple. He lifted his split-bamboo sword to strike the decisive blow....

Bolan moved so fast that Benkei did not see the forward lunge. The big foreigner pulled the thrust, but the point of his sword was pressing lightly on the other man's throat protector.

"Yame," called Yumoto. The bout was over.

"You show a natural aptitude for the sword." Yumoto congratulated Bolan in the changing room as the Westerner discarded the unfamiliar robes. They were alone.

Yumoto had iron-gray hair, cut very short. He was about sixty. "These recruits they send me do not grasp the essence of the sword. It is no longer relevant to their work as bodyguards and the like. But one does not study it to learn how to kill, rather it is to submit to a moral discipline.''

Bolan nodded. He understood.

''With formal training, Colonel, you could be very good—perhaps one day a master.''

''I am not worthy to receive such a compliment,'' Bolan replied.

The rough old man was won over by the American's modesty; that, too, was a virtue in short supply these days.

They talked about the various training methods that Yumoto employed to get the recruits into shape for their potentially dangerous assignments. Many traditional weapons were used to improve the men's timing and their reaction speed.

Yumoto laughed when Bolan asked him about *ninja* techniques, not because he took their visitor to be yet another thrill seeker, but at the thought of trainees like the just-defeated Benkei mastering the skills of the black warriors.

''The *ninja* practice walking across taut rice paper until it can bear their weight without making a single tear in the paper. With small grappling hooks sewn into their suits they can climb smooth walls. The *ninja* use *sai-min-jutsu*—'' Yumoto searched for the right word in English ''—the power of the mind....''

''Hypnosis?''

''*Hai.* Hypnosis. Some people think they are wizards. There are few men left who know the secrets of the *ninja*. No, Colonel, we do not teach such things here.''

Bolan could have spent a lot longer with Yumoto,

and he apologized for having to leave. Even as Yumoto escorted him to the gymnasium door, the instructor was still ruminating on his favorite topic. "These young men do not grasp its importance, for to understand the art of the sword is to understand the strategy underlying any confrontation. I shall retire soon, I think. They have no use for the sword."

That was an unjust conclusion, thought Bolan, as he walked over to rejoin Suki. What with chopping their fingers off and committing ritual suicide, Yumoto's countrymen still seemed to find plenty of use for the sword.

"If I DIDN'T KNOW yours was a government agency," Bolan said to Nakada, as Suki showed him into the latter's office, "I'd think you were training a private army down there."

The commander lighted another cigarette, although a butt was still smoldering in the ashtray. He appeared unamused at Bolan's offhand remark.

Bolan stared down from the rain-streaked window—Nakada's office was located in one of the gingerbread mansion's two towers—and he could see the trainees doubling around the edge of the lawn.

"Did you see the car?" asked Nakada. "It's built like a tank."

"I noticed it when we parked."

"Perhaps we can take it for a test run tomorrow," offered Nakada. "That is, if I can wrap up this Ikida affair. We finally got a break. It is very difficult to find an informer in this country."

Bolan nodded, remembering the stories of the *ninja* who would certainly die rather than risk being forced to talk.

A woman walked into the office, carrying several files and a slip of paper. She was apparently Nakada's secretary. He looked up, and she addressed him in rapid Japanese.

"Some more information on those men who attacked us," explained Nakada, glancing at the neatly scripted message. "The local police identified the body. He was a small-time hoodlum who soldiered for one of the families. But our records indicate he had a brother who was jailed for demonstrating against America's nuclear deterrent. I hardly think that connection has anything to do with last night."

Bolan shrugged.

The secretary brought other files to Nakada's attention. "This is the itinerary for the German foreign minister's visit. These are the preliminary floor plans for the new banquet hall in Osaka...."

She flipped open the last folder and placed it in front of Nakada. He picked up the top paper, a neatly typed report, and Bolan found himself staring across at a familiar face.

The picture clipped to a thin sheaf of papers was that of the older man in Shinoda's photographs.

There was no mistaking that odd streak of white hair.

10

Suki drove Bolan back alone, Nakada staying behind to catch up on his work. The traffic was much busier on the way into the city, and Bolan took his time to steer the conversation to the subject that interested him: the report he had seen Nakada sign.

"Professor Naramoto was one of our most brilliant scientists, though his work was not publicized. He'd been with the Red Sun Chemical Company for years, so his disappearance is most mysterious," Suki told him. It did not sound as if she felt the case should have been closed.

"What happened?"

"A boating accident." Again, Suki hesitated. "Apparently. Could I have one of those?"

Bolan lighted them each a cigarette and waited for her to continue.

"He chartered a small power-cruiser for a day... took his wife with him...then they vanished, boat and all."

"How long ago was this?"

"About a month. Down by the Umishi peninsula. It's a beautiful area. Red Sun has a company retreat there for their senior employees. Frogmen have searched along the coast, but they found nothing."

"Nothing at all?"

"It's a very rough shoreline with hidden rocks and

powerful currents. The local police called on Commander Nakada's services—at the insistence of Red Sun, I should add—but after the underwater search proved fruitless, he concluded the boat must have got into trouble, probably hit a rock and sank immediately.''

"And so the professor and his wife are presumed to have drowned?''

"Yes, Colonel, that's what it says in the final report.''

"But what do you think?''

Suki did not reply for a moment, making a fast lane change to overtake a truck.

"I think it was unwise of the professor not to have taken along a younger man to crew the boat.''

They were getting close to the hotel. Bolan asked Suki to join him for dinner, thinking he might extract more useful information over a warm flask of sake. Suki considered his invitation. It really seemed as if she wanted to say yes, but then she claimed she had a prior engagement.

Bolan lingered for a moment as he got out of the car, but she did not change her mind. He could not tell if her reluctance was for professional or personal reasons.

He watched the car drive off. Whatever her motives, Suki remained quite mysterious.

Bolan prowled the restless streets.

Perhaps it was better this way. He was glad to be on his own. It gave him time to think things through as he walked with a purposeful stride in an unspecified direction. Not even the crowds that thronged the sidewalks, nor the dazzling display of

Tokyo's fluorescent advertising, could distract him.

He was back in the jungle of the street.

Where The Executioner was born.

Where he was forged.

Where he belonged.

And where that sixth sense now told him he was being followed.

Bolan had expected Nakada might put a tail on him. After all, the commander could not take the risk that any more trouble should plague such an influential guest. Anticipating this, Bolan had taken every precaution after leaving the hotel. The thin man with tinted glasses and a raincoat folded over his arm was left behind in a large department store on the Ginza. In a city as overcrowded as Tokyo it was really not too hard to shake off a tail, but the crowds made it far more difficult to spot one.

Assuming the air of a slightly bewildered tourist, the tall American paused outside a diner apparently to inspect the plates full of plastic food that advertised the menu.

He picked her out on the second sweep. In a bobbing sea of black hair, she stood out as a blonde. It was the woman from the airport, the one with glasses and her hair tied in a bun.

She was standing by a newspaper kiosk, seeming to browse through the latest edition of *Time*, but to Bolan's experienced eye it was obvious she was more interested in the nearby entrance of a *pachinko* parlor.

Bolan moved to the doorway of a travel agency. He took his time lighting a cigarette, watching her as she fidgeted with another magazine. There was no doubt that she was the woman who had been arguing with the immigration officials at the airport. She glanced nervously around the street. To avoid any chance of eye contact, Bolan turned to face the window.

The travel agency was selling escorted tours of Japan's perennial attractions. A series of posters advertised visits to Mount Fuji, the giant bronze statue of the Great Buddha at Nara, and to Osaka by the superexpress "bullet" train. What caught Bolan's attention was the colored photo of a thatched building—the same cottagelike shrine that was featured in Shinoda's snapshots.

It was used to illustrate a guided tour of the Shinto shrines in the Umishi area. Maybe in the morning Colonel Phoenix would take up Suki's offer to do a little sightseeing. It was time he made a pilgrimage of his own.

Bolan almost missed the guy coming out of the pinball arcade.

It was Pock Face! Bolan caught the white flash of his bandaged hand where Suki had skewered him with her hairpin. And the second fellow, the weaselly looking one in the ill-fitting shiny suit, could be the one who had given the orders last night—Bolan was willing to bet he had a mouthful of gold teeth.

What the hell was a young female American visitor doing shadowing those two hoods?

They strutted down the block, and the woman took off after them. Bolan followed on his side of the street.

The unwitting game of three-way hide-and-seek threaded its way past several twenty-four-hour coffee shops, a couple of porno movie houses, a group of Japanese punk rockers who were even more bizarre than their Western counterparts, and a row of electronics and stereo stores engaged in a price war.

The two gangsters stopped to talk with an overpainted hooker. There was no sign that they realized they were being tailed.

Faced with the obstacle of a new shopfront construction, Bolan decided it was time to cross over. The big warrior felt a surge of energy as he dodged through the traffic.

Pock Face and his pal had vanished at the far end of the block. Bolan could see the young woman linger for a moment before turning right to follow them. He had to hurry if he was going to keep up.

When Bolan turned into the narrower side street, all three had disappeared. He brushed aside a foulbreathed pimp who clutched at his arm. He increased his pace. Dark alleyways led off at either side—they could have gone down any one of them.

He turned to make sure he had not already passed the woman hiding in one of the shadowy doorways. Then he heard the scream.

It came from a dark alleyway. Bolan pushed past a businessman bargaining with a B-girl and plunged into the alley. It ran round the back of a dingy butcher shop. The place stank of rotting garbage.

"If you dare try anything...." The voice was frail, breaking on the far edge of desperation.

The woman had her back to a brick wall and was holding a pair of sharp nail scissors in her outstretched hand. It was an inadequate weapon, but it temporarily held her opponents at bay.

There were now four of them: Pock Face, Gold Teeth and two young thugs sporting elaborate tattoos. They shifted around in a loose semicircle, seeing who would be first to risk a poke in the eye.

Bolan called out calmly, "Leave her alone."

He walked up to her, turned deliberately to face them with one arm held protectively across the woman's front.

Gold Teeth looked past him and nodded a quick signal. Bolan shifted just far enough to see a fifth soldier approaching with a stout length of wood in his hands.

A *yakuza* street gang versus The Executioner.

Five against one.

The odds were about even.

As the newcomer jumped in, hefting the shaft, Bolan unleashed a powerful side kick that caught the attacker in the solar plexus. Even as he turned to counterbalance, the big man took advantage of his long reach to punch Tattoo One, who sprang in from the other side.

The decorated youth might as well have run head-first into the wall. Skin split and nose gristle tore as his face was flattened into a blood-spurting mask.

Bolan ducked low, dodging under a high kick from Tattoo Two, and snatched the wooden club from the first guy, who was still retching his guts out.

"Thanks," snarled Bolan as he grasped the weapon and straightened up, bringing it around in a hard, tight swing. In Yankee Stadium it would have been a homer in the left-field stands for sure, but there was no ball to connect with, just the third punk's ribs.

Beneath his nylon shirt, a tattooed butterfly almost flew into the punk's lung cavity. The guy went down.

The blonde staggered against the wall for support. In those final seconds before the hoods closed in on her, she had tried to make a deal with God—but she had not anticipated that He would send a cross between a white knight and an executioner.

Pock Face tripped over the guy with the mangled rib cage in his haste to escape. His bandaged hand smacked down on the stones to break his fall, and Bolan slashed his club down on the hand with such force it shattered the guy's knuckles.

Gold Teeth ran off with a terrified yelp, hoping to escape before this bloodcrazed madman drove the precious bridgework down his throat.

Bolan grabbed the woman by the arm and hustled her down the alleyway. He did not look back at the carnage but hit the street and hailed a cab.

"I...I don't " she stammered as her savior bundled her into the rear seat. "Oh, thank God you came when you did!"

"Lady, you and I are going to have a little chat."

11

"Now, what the hell were you following those men for, Sandy?"

Her name was Sandra Dawson. Her small rented apartment was furnished with a minimum of second-hand pieces. Bolan was sitting cross-legged on a large cushion. He expected this sparsely decorated room to look out onto some sort of Zen rock garden instead of just another aging residential block.

"What are you doing here?"

"You will stay for tea, won't you?" Sandy turned away awkwardly before those icy eyes sliced right through her.

"I'm not going anywhere until I've got some straight answers out of you."

"Okay, but you know *my* name—what's yours?"

"Phoenix. John Phoenix."

"I'm a student, John Phoenix. I'm working on my doctoral thesis. Japanese history." Sandy paused to ladle the tea leaves into the pot. "My very first year I took an elective in Film Studies—it was all the rage then—you know, Kurosawa, Ozu, Mizoguchi...."

Bolan did not share a passion for Japanese cinema, but he nodded anyway.

"I got hooked. After that I specialized in Japanese history, politics, culture. By the time I completed my master's degree, I'd managed to pick up the language. At least, enough to get by.''

"I overheard you at the airport," Bolan said. She was astonished. ''You told those officers it was the third time you'd been here. . . .''

"That's right. You seem to have observed rather a lot of my crises lately. And risked your life for me, too. Well, I'm researching my dissertation," she said nervously. Then she relaxed. "I'm studying the period leading up to World War II. I'm trying to figure out the real power structure that brought Japan into the war. It's a story that's never been told.''

Now she was torn between the desire to share the excitement of her research and the need for secrecy. But since this brave man was already involved, to her mind there was no point in hiding her ideas from him. Besides, it might encourage him to pool his information with her.

"Have you ever heard of the Eight Jonin?"

Bolan shook his head.

"Very few people have," she said, warming to her subject as she poured out the tea. "The Eight Jonin are a select group of warrior-lords who have represented the true power in Japan for nearly two hundred years. They pushed their country into World War II. And they may still exist.''

Bolan sipped the hot greenish brown liquid from the little porcelain bowl.

"They control a fanatical organization called the Circle of the Red Sun," she continued.

"I've heard of Red Sun Chemicals.''

"A name that was not chosen at random, as a matter of fact. The Red Sun Chemical Company was owned by the Yamazaki family. My research will prove that Colonel Yamazaki was the Eighth Jonin throughout the thirties. He was their ringleader.''

"And only a colonel?" Bolan wore a slightly cynical smile. He had heard many conspiracy theories before.

"I'm being quite serious, John." Sandy's fingers reached for the small gold cross that nestled in her cleavage, as if she wanted to touch something to swear by.

She had long been immersed in her research and seemed unprepared for any sarcasm about it.

"Do you know how Red Sun got started?" she persisted. "I'll tell you. Government contracts before and during the war. They developed the germ strains used at the Unit 639 laboratory for bacteriological warfare that the Japanese ran in Manchuria. The testing facility there was under the command of Colonel Yamazaki. He didn't need a higher rank—he already gave the orders the generals listened to—and it was better not to draw attention to himself. But it didn't matter. Thanks to some POW's testimony, we got him anyway. Yamazaki was tried, found guilty and executed for war crimes in 1946.''

"And who took over the company? Did he have a son?"

"Yes. Hideo Yamazaki. But when he came of age, he handed over his holdings into trust and retired to a monastery."

"In reaction to his family's past?"

"I suppose so," she said, looking at him with bright, sad eyes. "The research team was headed by a Professor Naramoto."

"I know about him. He just died."

Sandy looked at Bolan even more closely. "His death didn't get much coverage considering how important he was. What's your interest in this, mister big guy? Are you a spy? That's it, isn't it, you're an industrial spy?"

"I try to *stop* industrial espionage." Bolan looked her straight in the eye. She was forced to glance down at her teacup.

She was better pleased with his answer than with her own suggestion. He had appeared as a knight in shining armor, and she would not have wanted him to be involved in anything that might tarnish that, even though she could sense the dangerous undercurrents that stirred in him. They stirred something in her, too.

"I think Naramoto's disappearance is the handiwork of the gang led by Kuma. His stepfather was also one of the Jonin," she said.

"Were those Kuma's men who cornered you tonight?"

"Yes," she nodded, her shoulders shivering at the thought of how close she had come to a bloody death. "Kuma started out as a sumo wrestler. It's always been his first love. He made a fortune in the black market and rose through the ranks of the *yakuza*. Now he heads the Kuma-*kumi*. Do you have any idea what a *capo di tutti capi* is?"

"Why, yes..." Bolan hesitated, smiling slightly. "Doesn't it mean 'the boss of bosses'? It's been a long time since I saw that movie."

"Brando's character was a pussycat compared to this guy," Sandy insisted innocently. "Some of the less scrupulous corporations use the *yakuza* as enforcers—you know, strong-arm men. They can help break up any industrial disputes, intimidate the competition, anything. Well, I think there's a close connection between Red Sun and the Kuma clan. It's the last piece in the puzzle that will show how the power of the Jonin still exists, that the same secret circle still exerts its evil influence. It'll bring my thesis right up to date.''

"And help sell a million copies?" Bolan smiled. Her enthusiasm was infectious, although the targets of her curiosity were of the dangerous kind. Fatally dangerous.

"I've been finding out a lot," she continued. "Remember the one with the gold teeth? He's one of Kuma's right-hand men. More of a messenger boy than muscle. I've been following him as best I can, keeping tabs on whom he makes contact with. Sooner or later, I'll prove the connection they have with Red Sun.''

Bolan thought she was damned lucky to have got as far as she had without being hurt. "This Kuma character—is he a big guy? A very big guy, maybe late forties, with the top of his little finger missing?"

"Yes, that's right. He did that to prove his loyalty to Kakuji. Actually, it was the only way he could get close to the old boss with a deadly weapon. Two minutes after chopping off his finger he stuck the sword through Kakuji and hacked up his bodyguards. That's how he became the boss of bosses.''

"Where are his headquarters?"

"He lives in a guarded penthouse on the top of the Nagana building. It's on the edge of the Shinjuku district. That's the fortress from which he runs his empire.''

Bolan could only gaze at her with concern and admiration. "I hope your supervisor knows what you're up to. You get full marks for risking your fool head, I guess."

He stood up to leave. Sandy appeared to be over her fright. In fact, there was now a wistfully romantic look in her eyes.

"You're not going, are you?" She stood up, too, as if to bar the way. "You haven't told me what you're up to."

"I never said I would," Bolan replied. "But you've put a lot of this together yourself, so I'll tell you one thing. There is a connection between Red Sun and Kuma's gang. Somebody obtained photographic evidence of that fact very recently."

"Where is it? Who's got it? Would they let me use it?"

"The guy can't." Bolan stared at her intently. "He's dead."

12

It was time to go for the jugular.

And the only place to start was right at the top—
the penthouse of the Nagana building. Bolan was going to track down the leader of the Kuma-*kumi* in his
lair.

Sandy had driven him back to the hotel in a bat-
tered Datsun borrowed from a Japanese friend. For
the moment Bolan hoped his cautionary tale would
make her think twice before proceeding with any
more detective work. She belonged in a library, sift-
ing through old records and correspondence, not out
on the streets chasing hoods. That was The Executioner's preserve.

Bolan used a service entrance to enter the hotel. He
picked up the few pieces of very special equipment
that had been hidden in his custom-designed briefcase, then left by the same unwatched exit and hailed
a cab to take him to the Shinjuku district.

Bolan got out at the railway station. There was no
sign of the man with the gold-rimmed glasses, but
still the American took a devious route through the
late-night passengers milling on the concourse,
through the washroom and past a buffet before he
was certain that no one would be following him.

Sandy's directions were straightforward. It took
him less than ten minutes to reach the Nagana build-

ing. It was twenty-six stories high, between an international airline company and a multi-floored Western-style boutique. It had lots of tinted glass, chrome, smooth stonework and was mostly used to house the dignified offices of a number of diverse subsidiaries—no doubt controlled, guessed Bolan, by the Red Sun Corporation.

He scouted the terrain.

Two guys were in a car parked across from the front entrance. The long antenna indicated they were in radio contact with other guards. Two more, in dark blue uniforms, were stationed in the brightly lighted lobby. They all looked the same: big, mean, and alert.

Bolan slipped into the alley beside the airline offices. A small driveway crossed behind the buildings, and a concrete ramp sloping down between two stout walls led to the underground parking lot beneath the Nagana building. The red glow from a cigarette gave away the position of a fifth sentry posted in the darkness.

He looked up at the apartment on the roof. The lights were on up there. Bolan could see a window-cleaning platform hanging from its hoists and silhouetted against the sky. Too bad it was secured to stay immobile at the top of the building.

He completed a full circle and stood in the shadows of a bank building. Through the big glass windows he could see one of the uniformed guards stand up and straighten his tunic before turning to watch the elevator doors open. Gold Teeth emerged, exchanged a few words with the goons on watch and headed for the front doors.

So the messenger boy had made his report. Now

the big boss knew about the two interfering foreigners. Good, thought Bolan, it would save him
from having to introduce himself.

He couldn't help but wonder how Gold Teeth had
embellished his account. He did not appear to have
any fingers missing.

A car drew up outside. A smooth operator, with
slicked-back hair and a sharply styled suit, hauled
out and hustled a young girl across the pavement.
Bolan judged she could not have been older than
fourteen. The pimp had his hand firmly clamped
round her upper arm as he steered her toward the
front door.

Gold Teeth passed them on his way out. He said
something to the man and turned to stare after the
girl as she was taken inside. He was wearing a wolfish
grin as he strolled over to his own car.

Bolan retraced his steps to the back of the building. There was no sign of the guard.

That made the big warrior doubly cautious. He did
not believe he could get so lucky.

Pulling the Beretta—the beautiful one-handed
automatic from Italy—out of its customized leather
hidden under his arm, Bolan dodged across the alley
and crouched behind the wall that flanked the garage
entrance.

A small stone rattled on the other side of the wall.
Someone's feet shuffled. Bolan froze.

Then he smelled it. The night breeze carried the
scent of marijuana drifting up from the ramp. The
guard had ducked out of sight to smoke a joint—anything to relieve the boredom.

Silently, very slowly, the deathshadow leaned over
the top of the wall.

The *yakuza* sentry, a hoodlum, indefensible, was propped against the stone directly below him. His fingers were squeezed around the roach as he concentrated on getting the last few drags of smoldering grass.

His dereliction of duty was going to cost more than a finger.

Bolan lowered his arm. The cough of the gun was masked by a passing motorbike.

A spurt of blood and bone chips streaked the sloping concrete as the hood's lifeless body buckled at the knees and tumbled down the ramp.

Bolan swung himself over the wall. The guard stared up at the starlit sky with only half a face.

Tough on you, guy, thought The Executioner, *but tonight is the night,* every *night. You should have known that.*

The man in black found the key in the sentry's pocket, fitted it in the electronic lock, then ran back to slip under the opening garage door.

Half a dozen cars were parked overnight. There was a scarred metal door between two concrete pillars at the far end. It led into the maintenance area.

Bolan threaded his way through mops and pails, floor polish and drums of lubricant, then past a workbench. He reached two narrow doors at the back of the janitor's cubbyhole. The beam of his pocket-size flashlight revealed the first of the other rooms to be full of electrical panels. The second door opened into the bottom of the elevator shaft.

The elevator car was suspended about twenty feet above his head, no doubt left at the ground-floor level by Smoothie after he'd delivered the girl to his boss.

Bolan began to climb toward it. By standing on top of the inside frame of the basement doors, he could reach the floor of the elevator. A quick flash from the torch revealed a service trapdoor on the bottom, flush with the metal of the underside, half hidden by the mess of hanging cables and rods under the car.

The big man stretched out and got a grip on the stoutest of the metal bars. Then he clipped onto one of the cross-struts a rubberized retaining shackle, connected to a lightweight safety wire, almost filament thin, that he wore in a reel on his belt. Once in place, he swung out into the center of the shaft.

In one hand-pull up the wire, Bolan was hanging right below the elevator floor hatch.

The elevator doors suddenly opened with a hum and a click. Male footsteps thundered immediately above his head.

It was too late for retreat. Cables whirred and the elevator was pulled upward, taking Bolan with it. He sacrificed the flashlight for a firmer hold with two hands. The little cylinder tumbled down the shaft in a brief frenzy of shattered light.

The elevator car shot to the top of the shaft. Must have been another message for the boss. Bolan glanced down past his feet: the well at the bottom was lost in darkness.

The elevator door opened and the occupant stepped out. The guy used a locking key of some kind to hold the elevator; the door did not shut again. There was a muffled sound as he called out for Kuma.

Well, he had not come along for the ride just to be taken all the way back to the basement again. Bolan was feeling the strain of hanging over a twenty-six story drop as he reached up to open the small trap-door. He unhitched the safety hook and squeezed through into the elevator car.

He peered around the corner of the open door. The plushy carpeted hallway was empty. Bolan could hear the low murmur of men's voices from a room at the far end of the apartment. He ran across the corridor and through a half-open door to a large kitchen.

Bolan decided against using a walk-in storage cupboard as a temporary refuge; instead, he worked his way in behind the American-brand vacuum cleaner in an adjacent closet.

He had just closed the door when Kuma and the guard walked past the kitchen. The gangster boss seemed to dismiss his retainer with a harsh order.

Bolan eased the door open a fraction. Kuma, dressed only in a short silk robe, was concentrating on what he could find in the refrigerator. Shinoda's photographs had been misleading: Kuma was not simply bigger than his fellow countrymen—the ex-sumo wrestler was enormous.

The bulky giant found some cold meat, bit off a chunk and padded back to his inner sanctum.

Kuma was going to need some persuasion to tell Bolan what he needed to know.

A thin sliver of light still shone from behind the refrigerator door. The Japanese gangster had not shut it properly. Bolan opened it a little more for greater visibility. He selected a broad-bladed chef's knife from the wall display. He placed it gently over the stove's biggest element and turned the knob to high. As he was closing the big refrigerator door,

Bolan noticed a plate of puffer fish sitting on the top shelf. Kuma evidently enjoyed the dangerous delicacy of *fugu*.

The American nightfighter set out to explore the next room.

It was Kuma's office.

The whole apartment was sumptuously furnished with heavy imported pieces. A gleaming rosewood desk stood close to the darkened window, probably so that Kuma could look out over the streets of Shinjuku and feel a sense of his own respectability.

There were a few papers on the desktop blotter. He saw a newspaper clipping held down by a weighty paper knife. It was a photograph torn from a Tokyo daily. Bolan recognized one of the men posed near the side of the group: it was Professor Naramoto, who had so recently drowned. At the other end of the line, ringed by a red felt-tip marker, stood the younger man with the glasses who was featured in Shinoda's snapshots. Bolan folded the picture carefully and tucked it in his pocket.

He could not risk using the gun. Anything might happen, and he wanted Kuma alive. Bolan undid his belt and extracted the short doubled loop of braided wire that it concealed. He paused for a moment to center his concentration, then stepped back into the passage.

He waited outside the entrance to the lounge. A contented grunting came from the room. Bolan risked a look.

The girl had been tied down, and most of her was hidden by the vast bulk of Kuma's body. He lay on top of her, hips rocking, as he forced himself into her.

Suppressing cold fury, Bolan crossed the room in six silent steps. The garrote was looped round Kuma's throat in a fraction of a second. The Executioner jammed his knee into the gangster's kidneys and gave the wire a savage jerk.

Kuma collapsed backward, his fingers scrabbling to find a hold on the thin band of metal that choked off any hope he might have had to bellow for help.

Bolan plucked his knife from its sheath as he kept hold of the garrote, and he moved slightly to slash the girl's bonds.

Kuma had fought too many bouts to lose on the first strike. A leg as thick as a tree trunk swept Bolan's feet out from under him. The knife flew uselessly from Bolan's hand. The fat man fell on him, pinning the American to the carpet. Kuma was still choking, more with rage than from the loosened garrote. His eyes were bulging with an uncontrollable fury.

Bolan managed to roll slightly to one side as a hamlike hand chopped for his throat. He took the blow on his shoulder.

The girl stood naked, a bewildered expression on her face. Her open lips were like a red wound. Bolan, his shoulder throbbing with the pain inflicted by the heavy hand, hollered quick instructions to the girl.

"Run. Get the hell out of—"

His words were choked off as Kuma locked a rippling forearm around Bolan's neck, squeezing with the power to kill. Bolan kicked out with his legs but could gain no leverage.

The Executioner, battling for breath and fighting for his life, saw the girl grab a tablecloth to cover her nakedness and run to a door. She had obviously understood his instructions.

Bolan, short of oxygen, felt the blood pulsating in his head. With a violently strong upswing, he brought his right forearm and wrist in a thrust over his shoulder, to jab at the greasy giant's eye. He drove his forefinger behind him into the socket. Kuma howled in pain and Bolan wriggled free.

His battle strategy already mapped out, the big guy leaped across the room and grabbed a brass poker.

Kuma saw the poker—but only with one eye—as it came lancing across his face.

When Kuma came to, he found he had been tied securely to the heavy teak dining table by the same cords he had used on the girl. He shook his head groggily.

"Okay, Mr. Big, you're going to answer some questions." Bolan kicked the fat guy's foot. It produced a grunted response. "See this picture?" Bolan leaned forward. "Who is this guy? What happened to Professor Naramoto? Why was Ken Shinoda killed?"

Kuma sneered, spat at his attacker. The wet missile missed Bolan and hit the carpet.

"No time for samurai heroics, Kuma," Bolan said. "I'm heating up a little something for you in the kitchen."

There was fear in Kuma's eyes; he was a man who recognized Bolan as a master. Bolan could see the terror of the unknown reflected there, and he turned away from the immobilized fat man and went to the kitchen.

The element was glowing orange red; the knife blade was the same color. He picked the knife up with a wad of rags and returned to the lounge.

The blade glowed like a branding iron. Its hot light

stabbed before him, penetrating the air, pulsing toward the stubborn slob.

Kuma's chin had sunk to his chest. His lips were compressed as if in anticipation of the pain to come.

"Yeah," said Bolan, "this is happening to *you*, Kuma. And it's going to get worse." The blade sizzled against the bristles on the man's oily chin rolls.

Yet Kuma gave no sign that he was willing to talk about anything. Bolan bent lower. "Let's start off with your connection with Red Sun."

Kuma judged the *gaijin* was within range. He looked up, spat again. This time it was red, bright red.

A spray of blood hit Bolan as the rubbery tag that had once been Kuma's tongue bounced off his shoe. The big fighter—the *capo di tutti capi* of Nippon— had bitten off his own tongue rather than talk. Rivulets of crimson dribbled from the sides of his mouth.

Bolan was cool, calm and enraged.

As he returned to the kitchen, Bolan understood that the gang war this would ignite might be explosive enough to dislodge the answers that he wanted. Bolan opened the refrigerator door.

The blood-drenched Kuma tried to keep his mouth clamped shut as Bolan walked back toward him.

"You cheated me, Kuma." Bolan slapped the *yakuza* chieftain hard, hard enough to make Kuma open his mouth to spit out more blood and gulp for air. "Here's something to shove in your mouth!"

In his other hand Bolan carried one of the cold clammy *fugu* fish. He rammed it between the gangster's parted lips.

The *yakuza* boss spluttered, trying to spit out the deadly creature. Bolan brought his hand up under the other man's jaw, forcing Kuma to bite down on the toxic puffer fish. "You should always chew your food before you swallow it."

It took only a matter of moments for the poison to work. Kuma writhed, coughed, then with a convulsive shudder he died. Once again his face was tight-lipped.

Bolan went back to the kitchen to clean himself of the blood and fish parts disgorged by the dying Kuma. He made sure he had the newspaper clipping, then Bolan walked out onto the small penthouse patio at the rear. A broad ledge ran along the side of the building. He moved onto it and strolled along to the window-washer's platform. It took a moment to figure out the controls.

He calmly released the platform and let himself down to the ground.

13

SHE OPENED THE DOOR as far as the chain would allow, saw it was the man she knew as John, then shut it again to remove the security lock. Bolan was pleased to find that Sandy was at least taking the basic precautions.

"What time is it?" she yawned, ushering him quickly inside. She wore a lightweight wrap with a bold Japanese ideogram embroidered on the back. With her hair down and no glasses to overshadow her gray green eyes, she looked very different.

"Early. It's early."

She did not ask him where he had come from or why he had shown up again at this hour. Sandy assumed there were certain rules to follow if you got mixed up with a special investigator.

Bolan handed her the newspaper clipping in exchange for another cup of her slightly bitter tea. He pointed to the face which had been ringed in red. "Recognize him?"

"No," Sandy shook her head slowly. "No, I don't. But that one there—third from the left—that's Professor Naramoto. There's no mistaking him. He had an accident in his homebuilt lab when he was just a schoolboy; it left him with that streak of white hair."

Bolan touched her shoulder. "How do you know

all this? You can't have found out all these details from old documents in libraries.''

"I've got my sources," she said with a theatrically mysterious air. "I have quite a few friends over here. In fact, I deliberately led one guy on to get the information I wanted. That's one of the reasons I left Japan for a while. Just to cool things off.''

Sandy felt a little better for having confessed, though she did not want this man to get the impression she was someone who used people.

"How many of these 'friends' know you're back?''

"Just Jimmy. He's the guy who lent me his car. I've been trying to get settled in again. Haven't had time to contact anyone else.''

"I think you should stick close to home for a while, Sandy," Bolan warned her. "Lie low. Things are going to get pretty ugly out there. Now give me an envelope and some notepaper.''

"Sure.''

Her briefcase was bulging with a student's supplies.

Bolan wrote out a covering letter, then paperclipped it to the torn-out photograph and slipped it into the envelope. He really did not want to involve her further, but she was already in it up to her neck.

"Would you take this to the American Embassy first thing today, please? Give it to Paul Ryan. Personally, you understand.''

"Will there be a reply?''

"No, not immediately." For the transmission to reach Brognola and for him to send back the appropriate information might take an hour, might take more. "Then I want you to return here and stay in. Wait for me. I'll be back later.''

Sandy bit her lip. There were so many things she wanted to ask him. But it was more important to observe the rules.

"When I get back, we'll talk."

"Take care, John," she said, reaching out to touch his hand.

Bolan quickly squeezed her hand in parting. Now it was time to monitor progress on a gang war. He would wait for Commander Nakada to connect with him back at his quarters. Things would be hopping this day.

"You too, scholar girl." He smiled at the blond young American in the Japanese nightgown. "Don't get carried away with any more of this research, okay? It's a real world out there, and it bites with razor teeth. Our enemies are surrounding us, and they will draw blood like airborne piranha."

The girl shivered involuntarily, then stole a look into the cold eyes of this hard man and, connecting with his gaze, held it with her green eyes.

"I know that," she said. "You must come back."

"Bet on it," Bolan said and turned toward the door.

THE DOORMAN could not restrain a short gasp of surprise and respect, when the monstrous limousine stopped to pick Bolan up. The doorman touched two fingers to his forehead in salute as he opened the rear door for their American guest. He had not realized they had such an important man staying at the hotel.

"Commander Nakada said you would like to be taken along the Umishi coastline," said the driver.

"Yes, if that's possible."

The woman behind the wheel nodded. She did not

turn to give him Suki's smile. Bolan guessed she was another upwardly mobile female in Nakada's department.

Most of the taxis steered clear of the long, heavy car as it surged easily through the morning traffic. A couple of them raced alongside to see if they could recognize who was in the back. No one could see clearly through the smoked glass, but they tooted anyway, assuming that the passenger must be a visiting movie star.

Bolan was grateful that the driver did not want to talk. He let her concentrate on the road as he sank back into the softly padded pearl gray upholstery. It really was a very comfortable ride. Only thoughts of last night's bloody events unsettled the sensation of ease.

Kuma had not looked like the sort who would scare that quickly, and yet something had driven the *yakuza* boss to mutilate himself horribly rather than risk Bolan's questioning. Fanatical loyalty or abject fear? Bolan was too deep into the ties between a top gangster and the large chemical company to back off now.

The ties were like links in a chain. At one end were the bugs of World War II, the invisible assassins bred at Yamazaki's Unit 639; and at the other was Shinoda and the needed bacteria for his revolutionary biochip. Bolan would sniff out the man in the middle.

The Executioner rested, conserving his strength for the struggle ahead.

"That's one of the superexpresses, sir."

Bolan glanced out the window to see the sleek, aerodynamically designed "bullet" train. The limousine must have been cruising at eighty or faster, but the train was steadily overtaking them. The track banked away from the road, and Bolan lost sight of the railed projectile behind a swiftly looming hill.

"That train will arrive in Umishi at least twenty minutes before we get there," the driver informed him.

Much of the uneven land on either side of the road was terraced into tiers of rice fields. This was picture-postcard Japan. Then the soil dried out, became sandier, and the cultivated lots gave way to pine woods. Bolan saw a sign in three languages pointing the way to a hot-springs area.

It was another five minutes before he caught his first glimpse of the sea. The beaches were few and short and steep, and cliffs predominated, dropping sheer into the foaming swell. Out at sea the waves were choppy, indicating fierce undertows.

A few lonely boats braved the blue gray water.

"Pearl divers," explained the driver, not shifting her attention from the upcoming bends hugging the twisted contours of the coastal cliffs. Bolan was more interested in the tall towers he had caught sight of between the dark evergreens to the right.

"What's that place?"

"Shoki Castle. It was a castle, but now it's a kind of recreational center, an executive retreat owned by one of our major companies."

They sped past the high gates. There was no mistaking the logo on the sign outside, warning off uninvited visitors.

"Would that be the Red Sun Corporation?"

"Yes, sir. The Yamazakis have always treated their employees as one large family."

Bolan looked the other way at the sea pounding the base of the cliff below them.

"Wasn't it along this stretch of coast that Professor Naramoto disappeared?"

"I'm. . .I'm not completely sure of the exact location. Perhaps it was. I didn't work on that case."

Bolan lighted a cigarette to divert her attention from his look into the driving mirror. She was watching him, too, evidently interested in his reaction.

"Commander Nakada insisted that I demonstrate the major features of the car for you."

Bolan let her change the subject—he had something else on his mind.

She reached out with her left hand and touched a switch in the control panel. A shatterproof glass partition slid into place between them.

"That seals off the passenger compartment." Her voice sounded tinny through the small interconnecting speaker. She pushed another button. "And that electronically locks the rear doors."

Bolan was trying to place those eyes in the mirror.

"Nothing could get in to reach you, sir."

Pretty—in an unmemorable sort of way.

That's what he thought the first time he saw her.

She was the woman in the photographs.

But how. . .?

She turned slightly and glanced back over her shoulder. Her lips moved and the disembodied voice announced, "And it is impossible for you to get out."

She touched the brakes, and the car slowed as it approached the crest of the rise ahead. "We trust you'll enjoy the rest of the ride, Colonel Phoenix. Now I must leave you. . . ."

The woman opened the door and with practiced ease leaped out onto the grass verge.

Bolan smashed his fist against the glass.

It was useless.

The driver's door slowly swung shut as the car began to pick up speed. The road dropped for about two hundred yards, then turned sharply to the right. But there was no one at the wheel to handle the bend.

Bolan could see the cliff edge rushing toward him.

There was absolutely nothing he could do.

The heavy car hit the graveled shoulder, flattened the tussocks of salt grass and plunged over the cliff.

14

THE SLEEK AUTOMOBILE knifed through the water and submerged almost immediately, the weight of its thick, reinforced body armor dragging the vehicle toward the bottom.

Bolan collapsed in a heap against the solid glass partition, the breath knocked out of him, but his limpness an advantage in absorbing the impact.

The attack-proof compartment was sinking into an eerie gloom. A seething, silvery cloud of bubbles swirled past the windows.

Inside it was as silent as a tomb.

The resistance of the water slowed the car as it continued to drop nose first. Then the heavy automotive coffin bumped to a halt, wedged at a sloping angle with its front end trapped between two rocks. The engine had coughed its demise, but the ignition was still on, the dash lit by a solitary light.

Bruised and shaken, Bolan took his bearings. He was standing on the tilted shatter-resistant shield. The rear window was just above his head.

The final impact had not been enough even to bend the specially reinforced frame.

The doors held firm.

No water leaked into the interior.

It would probably still be dry when they winched up the vehicle and hauled his corpse from it.

Bolan assumed that was the plan. He wondered whose corpse they would substitute for the driver.

Would Suki be found in there with him? She, probably drowned, he asphyxiated? All along he had sensed that Suki wanted to tell him something. Now, he realized, she had wanted to warn him.

There was a small cut on his cheek. The skin had split when he had been slammed into the glass. The flesh already felt puffy. His knee ached from the twisted way he had been thrown around. But nothing was broken.

The surrounding shroud of air bubbles was breaking up. Only scattered trails of escaping air ascended as Bolan began, inch by inch, to examine his underwater cell. Looking up through the rear window, he judged he was stuck perhaps forty feet below the surface, considering the time it had taken to hit bottom.

A school of striped fish flitted past, found nothing to interest them, veered away in unison. The cloud of sand and debris was settling now. A cold twilight prevaded the sunken car.

For a brief moment he thought it was a shark coming to investigate.... Pale, golden, the shape rippled toward him. He had not yet exhausted the air, he could not be seeing things—but here before him was a mermaid.

The pearl diver was naked except for a pair of goggles. She was carrying a heavy steel crowbar of the kind used to pry tenacious oysters from their rock crevices. She wore no diving equipment.

Bolan watched as the woman swam gracefully through the deep.

She tapped the crowbar against the glass. Bolan

signaled toward the unlocked driver's door, jabbing with his finger and making a levering motion.

The unclad diver understood.

She tried and tried again. The pointed flange could find no purchase against the front window.

Bubbles of spent oxygen were leaking slowly from her nostrils. Bolan wondered how long she could possibly stay down here.

She pushed the end of the crowbar into the edge of the door, close to the handle, and applied one final burst of pressure.

Something gave. The metal buckled, and the door latch was giving.... The sea sprayed into the driver's compartment.

Bolan saw jets of salt water spout into the front of the car.

The diver banged the roof. Bolan watched her feet disappearing as she rose to the surface for a much-needed gulp of fresh air.

A new cloud of bubbles erupted from the car as the sea rushed in through the slight gap she had forced open by the catch.

Bolan watched... and waited.

The water level rose.

The multiple-control dash was swamped. Something zapped. The circuits shorted. The glass partition dropped a few inches, then stopped. The water could rise no farther because of the air trapped in the passenger section.

Bolan pushed down hard against the top edge of the glass partition. It slid open a little more—not all the way, but enough for him to climb through to the front.

The water was cold.

He kicked hard, and the front door opened a little. Bolan took in a deep breath from the space that had been intended as his grave, ducked under and eased himself through the half-open door.

The woman was coming down again to get him. Bolan entrusted himself to her guiding hands. When he looked up he saw the black cigar-shaped shadow of a boat above them. Even in his haste to escape from the steel box below, Bolan had the presence of mind to surface on the seaward side of the pearl-diver's boat, in case prying eyes were watching from the cliff top.

A grinning boatman helped haul Bolan over the gunwale.

The rescued warrior lay on a tarpaulin in the bottom of the boat, drinking in the sweet, cool air.

"Thank you," he gasped, sitting up between a bucket of oysters and a wicker basket half filled with crabs.

The woman swung herself up over the side of the wooden craft. Without a trace of self-consciousness at her nudity, she gave the American a sharp nod of her head. Bolan returned the bow.

"Bad spot. Two crash." The boatman held up two fingers to emphasize his point. "Car sink...boat sink."

"Where did boat sink?" Bolan asked forcefully. "You show me boat. Please."

The man turned to consult the diver. She shrugged. They could show him.

The man rope-started the ancient outboard, and they motored along under the cliffs, back in the direction of Shoki Castle. The men glanced up at the road. Bolan was watching for a sign of that treacherous driver; the boatman was checking the landmarks that would guide him to the earlier wreck.

The woman was the first to signal that they had arrived. Yet she had not lifted her eyes from the surface of the water. Her gaze seemed to penetrate the depths.

Bolan took off his shoes and jacket, seized a pair of goggles from the floor of the boat and followed her over the side.

The cruiser was not in as deep water as the car was. The fiberglass hull was balanced on a rocky ledge less than thirty feet below the surface.

It required a considerable effort to swim down against the strong current that must have pushed the boat onto its present precarious perch. Even now the stern was swaying gently, and Bolan guessed the next storm would push it off to sink in the deep, dark waters on the far side of the shelf.

There were no bodies to be seen. The predators that haunted these shores would have taken care of their disposal. The pearl-diving nymph circled, coming back to tap Bolan's shoulder. She pointed to the aft section. There was a long hole torn in the hull, below what would have been the waterline.

Bolan was almost at the limit of his lungs' endurance, but he swam closer to investigate.

The shredded edges of the gash splintered *outward*. If the professor had hit a sharp rock, the fiberglass skin would have been rammed inward. So it was from a force of some kind, a bomb, inside the engine compartment. The boat must have sunk immediately.

Bolan had seen enough. He signaled to the woman that he was going back up. He glanced toward the surface, saw the silhouette of the boat and slowly ascended.

"I take you back to shore," said the man. "My village not far." He made a sweeping motion to show that they were heading for a harbor in the cove around the point.

Bolan was slipping his shoes back on when he heard the heavy throb of a launch's powerful motor. He lay flat in the bottom of the boat and tugged the oil-stained tarpaulin over himself.

He took a quick glimpse over the edge of the canvas sheet and saw a converted patrol boat, flying the Red Sun company ensign, knifing through the waves. The pearl gatherers' dinghy rocked in the wash of the larger vessel, which passed close enough to inspect them.

The man at the tiller gave the uniformed sailors an amiably stupid grin, but as soon as they pulled away he spat over the side. The local fishing and pearl-diving folk were not part of the Red Sun's one big happy family.

15

THE PEARL DIVER had an older brother who was driving his fish truck to Tokyo. It was cramped in the small cab, and there was no escape from the briny stink of their cargo, but at least Bolan felt confident he would reach his destination in one piece.

The driver did not speak any English, which gave Mack Bolan time to think. He was still not sure if the woman who had tried to kill him had infiltrated Nakada's security squad without its leader's knowledge, or whether she had switched with the substitute driver that morning. But given the evidence of Naramoto's sabotaged boat, which the police and frogmen together, under Nakada's direction, could not find, Bolan was beginning to suspect that Nakada himself had given the orders for his watery disposal.

After a sign-language conversation including much patient repetition, Bolan got the truck driver to drop him off a block from Sandy's apartment. The man refused to accept any payment for the ride.

Bolan checked both ways before entering a side door that served as a fire exit.

"What happened to you?" Sandy asked as she unlocked the door. She was wrapped in the same thin robe she had worn that morning; tonight, blond ringlets clung to her neck. "You look a mess, John...."

Bolan shrugged.

"Run yourself a bath," she said. "I'll see if I can clean your clothes and press them a little."

Bolan did not argue. Another bath in one day was better than none.

"I've got some interesting news for you, John," she called out, as she plugged in the compact traveling iron she had bought on her previous stay in Japan. "Guess who Professor Naramoto really is!"

"Tell me."

"Saburo Naramoto was the youngest scientist to work in Manchuria during the war. Somehow he kept a low profile throughout the Occupation and Reconstruction period. But a friend told me that the respected Professor Naramoto began his career as Colonel Yamazaki's own protégé at the Unit 639 project."

"I thought I told you to stay put," Bolan said.

"You told me to stay in," protested Sandy. "You didn't say not to use the phone."

"Lying low means just that," Bolan called out from the bathtub. "Did you manage to see Paul Ryan?"

"Yes...and that reminds me, there's a package for you."

Bolan heard her cross over to the tiny kitchen. It was a couple of minutes before she opened the bathroom door.

Sandy was carrying a tumbler of Scotch—a peace offering for having bent the rules.

"I was saving this. Duty free. Real Scotch still makes a very worthwhile bribe in Japan." She handed him the drink and took the officially sealed envelope from under her arm. "Here. It's from

Ryan. I'll leave you to read it in peace, while I try to get a crease back into those pants.''

He took a single sip of whiskey, then ripped open the heavy envelope.

Ryan had returned the original clipping. It was stapled to a long teletype of a decoded message from Brognola. The man in Washington had already come up with the answers. The information was succinct. Bolan went through it point by point.

The thatched buildings had been identified definitively as a Shinto shrine on the southwestern tip of the Umishi peninsula. The two roped-together boulders—a smaller copy of the better known "Wedded Rocks" at Futamigaura—were on the beach below the holy buildings. It was less than an hour's drive from the area where the Shinoda family originally came from....

Yes, thought Bolan, *and only four or five miles from Red Sun's Shoki Castle.* If he had reached it, he might have done a little sightseeing there himself.

Brognola also told him that clearance had been obtained to inspect the details of Shinoda's private business affairs. The balance he maintained in the bank, plus the various investments he already held, indicated that Shinoda was too well off to stoop to blackmail. With some prudent rearrangement of his personal finances he could even have afforded to purchase Karl Brandt's beautiful yacht.

Bolan turned to the next page.

His hunch was confirmed.

The man in the photograph had been identified as Akira Okawa, a fellow scientist and Shinoda's rival in California. The group portrait had been taken recently at an international symposium of leading biochemists. It was held in Japan at the same time Kenji Shinoda had been on vacation there. And a voiceprint analysis, continued Brognola's teletype, suggested that the person who had been taped calling Shinoda might be—stress, *might be*—Okawa. The sample was not long enough for positive identification.

There was a separate sheet attached with some biographical details on Akira Okawa.

He was born in 1944 in Camp Alameda, where his parents, along with many other Americans of Japanese ancestry, had been interned for the duration of the war. His father had died there only weeks before they were released. Like Shinoda, Okawa had been a brilliant student from the beginning. But, spurning several lucrative government contracts, Okawa had carved out a comfortable niche for himself in private industry.

There was an additional note appended to this sketchy outline.

The Bear says that Okawa was probably the only scientist who could have provided the chemical knowledge to complement Shinoda's genius. But their antagonism toward each other was so bitter that there was little chance they could ever work together.

Not unless Shinoda found some leverage, noted Bolan, *like evidence of Okawa's contact with Japanese gangsters and business rivals.*

The last line of the typed communication read, "Striker, I think it's time we talked with Okawa. H.B."

Bolan folded the papers and stuffed them back into the envelope.

Sandy tapped once and stuck her head round the door. "Supper's ready when you are."

She had laid out an easy-to-fix meal on a low table in the main room.

"I did make some other calls today," she admitted as they sat across from each other, Bolan clad in freshly pressed pants.

"So what else did you find out?"

"Oh, that the Temple of the Eight Bells isn't all it appears to be." Sandy did a deliberately bad job of sounding offhand.

"And how does the Temple of the Eight Bells fit into all this?"

"In the spring of 1942, Colonel Yamazaki was on leave from Manchuria. His son, Hideo, was born in January 1943. The little boy never had the chance to know his father. Hideo was only three and a half years old when the colonel was shot for crimes against humanity."

Ask Sandy a simple question and you get a history lesson, noted Bolan.

"In 1964, Hideo Yamazaki surrendered his business inheritance and retired to the contemplative life. It was a significant gesture, but it was overshadowed by the excitement surrounding the Olympic Games. And he went into monastic retreat at the Temple of the Eight Bells."

Bolan was increasingly absorbed in thought as he served himself some rice.

Sandy continued, her chopsticks poised in midair. "The temple had been controlled for years by a very corrupt abbot, whose somewhat-less-than-spiritual appetites have long been catered to by the *yakuza*.''

"Specifically by Kuma.''

"Right again. My friend Jimmy, who told me all this, used to work for an art dealer who suspected that the temple had become a pipeline to Kuma's gang for a profitable supply of religious scrolls, paintings and rare sculptures.''

"I think it's time I paid a visit to Hideo Yamazaki.''

"You're going to the temple?''

"No,'' Bolan shook his head. "To Shoki Castle. Yamazaki may be living in retreat from the world, but I don't believe he's at that monastery.''

16

SANDY HAD quite a day to look forward to—she was driving John Phoenix down to Umishi.

"Would you call this number for me, please?" Bolan handed her a slip of paper from his waterproof wallet. The early-morning daylight streamed into the sparsely furnished apartment. "Ask for Setsuko Seki, or Suki."

"What if I get hold of her?" Sandy asked.

"Let me talk to her."

Sandy spoke to the switchboard operator in Japanese, waited for a moment, then repeated her request to someone else.

Bolan watched her cut off the connection by jabbing her finger down on the cradle. Whoever that was seemed very keen to know who was calling.

"Well?"

"She's not there right now. She's sick. They expect she'll be away for a few days."

He shook his head sadly, then drained the coffee. He had just suggested they start their drive when the phone rang. Sandy answered it. This time the conversation alternated rapidly between Japanese and English as she talked with mounting enthusiasm.

"That was Jimmy," she told him. "There's a man named Manutsu—he's an ex-wrestler, who's willing to talk to me. He's known Kuma from the days when they fought in the ring and there's no love lost between them. He'll be able to tell me a lot about the *obayum* of the Kuma-*kumi*. Jimmy tried to fix things before but got nowhere. Something must have happened, because suddenly Manutsu is willing to talk.''

Bolan knew what had happened, even if Sandy did not. He had made it happen. The gangster overlord was dead. It might not have been officially announced in the papers yet, but the news was obviously on the street.

''How are you to contact him?''

''He'll be at the sumo arena around noon. The apprentice matches will be under way, and there'll be two tickets waiting for us. We could go on to Umishi straight afterward.''

Bolan thought for a moment, then nodded. He, too, wanted to hear what this ex-wrestler character had to tell them about Kuma.

He used the extra time to go down to Sandy's bank on the corner to cash several traveler's checks. When he got back to the apartment there had been another call—this time for him.

''Mr. Ryan said it was most urgent,'' Sandy stressed. She padded into the bathroom to brush her hair and to give John a little privacy to return the call.

The intelligence liaison officer at the embassy had not yet been informed of Bolan's accident, but he had a brief message to relay from Brognola.

Akira Okawa was dead.

They had arrived at his home to find he had hanged himself in the garage. Foul play was not suspected.

Not suspected! Okawa may have committed suicide, thought Bolan, *but it reeked with the corrupt odor of conspiracy.*

It was time he made his play. The Beretta was holstered underneath a casual cream-colored Windbreaker.

"Let's go!" he called out to Sandy.

Although they left with plenty of time to get to the arena, it took them nearly twenty minutes to find a parking spot.

They entered through a long covered corridor lined with catering stalls. Sandy spoke to one of the men selling programs. He directed her to a guy wearing a flat cap and dark glasses. He was holding the complimentary tickets for her.

"He wanted to show us to our seats but I said no," explained Sandy as they walked away.

The narrow aisle leading down to the rows of little box seats on the main floor was congested with restless patrons and refreshment dealers. The great square hall could seat more than ten thousand. Now it was about one-third full.

"Nishiwaga." Sandy checked the ticket numbers. "On the western side. Must be over there."

Bolan looked down at the ring. Above it was suspended a wooden roof built in the traditional Shinto design. Two heavyset youngsters faced each other across the circular sanded arena. They clapped their hands and stamped fearsomely on the clay floor.

Sandy ran her eye along the row of boxes, each fenced off by a low aluminum railing, trying to spot Manutsu.

"That must be the one," she said, pointing out a balding man in his late forties, still big and not yet turned to blubber. She touched Bolan's hand. "Follow me, John."

They squeezed past people to get to the designated row.

The colorfully robed referee signaled with his fan for the bout to begin. The favored apprentice from the Oshiyama stable charged at his opponent. The Tomikaga novice smartly sidestepped, as much in sudden fear as for a tactical maneuver. The expected winner stumbled past in surprise and sprawled out of the ring.

The match was over.

The crowd was on its feet, shouting at this unpredicted turn of events that had enlivened, if also shortened, the routine preliminary bouts.

One man had not stood up.

Manutsu slumped dejectedly on his purple cushions.

"Keep moving," Bolan ordered the girl. "Don't stop!"

He almost had to push her past the back of Manutsu's box. The retired wrestler still had not moved. And Bolan knew he never would.

"Make for the other aisle," he said. Sandy struggled through the crowd.

"He must have had something very important to tell us," said Bolan, scanning the audience above them.

At the top of the steps three men in identical outfits—slacks, polo-neck sweaters, Windbreakers, all black—had almost reached the exit.

The one in the lead paused to turn, surveying his handiwork, double-checking the hit for the report he would have to make. He caught sight of the tall foreigner below him.

Their eyes locked in a hard-edged glare that cut across the heads of the crowd.

It was the man with the twisted lip.

Bolan nodded almost imperceptibly. His black-clad enemy did not misinterpret that faint sign of recognition. It was a matter-of-fact challenge that simply stated, let's be at it.

But the three strongmen swaggered anyway. They could not afford to be waylaid by the *gaijin*. Their master called.

"Zeko Tanga." Sandy heard Bolan utter the name like a low curse. Bolan began to weave his way up the aisle, taking the steps two at a time where he could. She had to hurry to keep up with him.

They were still in sight at the end of the covered foyer. All three were walking fast but not rushing headlong in flight—they did not want to attract undue attention to themselves.

As they approached the street, Bolan turned to Sandy. "You get the car. I'll keep after them on foot."

Sandy ran for the Datsun. Bolan watched her go, then turned to chase after Tanaga and his henchmen. He ran into a solid wall of flesh and muscle.

A giant wrestler grunted as Bolan knocked into him. The wrestler was used to respect from everyone when he visited the sumo hall—even from outsiders. This big Westerner would have to be taught a few manners.

Bolan could see this quarry escaping into the crowd on the opposite sidewalk, but the way was completely barred by the mountainous wrestler, who spread his paws out in a bearlike embrace.

There was no time for games. Tanga was getting away.

Bolan swallowed hard and gave the offended wrestler a deep bow.

All three hundred fifty pounds of the man quivered with suppressed rage: did this foreigner think he could get away with a stiff-necked apology?

Sandy got the car going on the third try. She could see the black-clad strongmen weaving through the spectators still coming to the stadium. Oh, God, John was in an argument with some gigantic wrestler!

The traffic lights changed. Sandy steered straight across the street, round a frightened noodle seller and mounted the sidewalk.

"John!" The brakes protested with a squeal as Sandy swung the Datsun broadside. Bolan jumped into the passenger seat, and she burned rubber across the paving, bumped over the gutter and accelerated into the traffic, giving two taxi drivers near heart attacks with her recklessness.

"They went this way!" Her voice was mounting with excitement. "Are you all right?"

Bolan nodded as he scanned the scurrying pedestrians ahead. He spotted the strongmen at the end of the next block. One of them had jumped off the sidewalk to flag down a taxi.

"I see them," said Sandy. The three men were bundling into a car ahead. She glanced across at Bolan with a wicked gleam in her eye. "Well. . . say it."

"Okay," said Bolan with a taut grin. "Follow that car!"

Sandy stepped on the gas, swerved past a panel truck and tore after the taxi.

A policeman dropped the whistle from his gaping mouth as the little Datsun screeched through a red light.

"Looks like they're heading for the train station," explained Sandy.

"I guessed as much. They've got a message to deliver."

She swung the wheel over hard, and the car slithered around the approach ramp to the station forecourt. Bolan began to open the passenger door. "I'm going after them."

"But what shall I—"

"We're going to Umishi, remember? I'll meet you there." Her knowledge of Japanese might prove even more useful than her rustbucket of a car.

"Where?"

There was no time for complicated directions. An image sprang to mind. "The hot springs, just off the main road, before you get to the castle."

Then he was gone.

Sandy pulled up a hundred yards behind the empty cab, but Bolan had already leaped from the car and was running into the main entrance. He vanished into the throng just disgorged by the Nagoya express.

Tanaga was smart. Not only would the "bullet" train get him back to home base far faster than any getaway car, but also the railroad station was the perfect place to elude any possible pursuit. That is, unless the pursuer knew where he was heading, as Bolan did. He brushed past the crowd looking for the train to Umishi.

It was waiting at the platform at the far end of the concourse.

Bolan dodged around a troop of nuns, squeezing between them and a locked ticket booth.

The hand came out of nowhere. Tanaga had left one of his buddies to deal with the interfering American. And the man knew his business.

Bolan spun around as the clawlike fingers dug into

his arm. The modern *ninja* had not expected the sudden fury that exploded on contact. Nothing was going to stop Bolan from reaching that train.

The loudspeakers announced the final call for the Umishi express.

Mack Bolan demolished the man from the ground up.

His heel smashed onto his adversary's foot, then he brought his knee up hard between the other guy's legs.

Crude but effective.

The soldier groaned, began to double over. Bolan grabbed his hair and pulled his head down to meet the other knee Bolan now brought pumping up into the man's face.

The warrior slumped onto the asphalt with a broken foot, his groin on fire, two teeth hanging by a shred, his nose mashed against his blood-spattered cheek, a curious high-pitched ringing in his ears. The American he should have stopped was off and running again.

Tanaga might have stood a better chance, but he could not risk a confrontation. Manutsu was dead, and the American just kept on coming. His presence in Tokyo must be reported.

Bolan caught a glimpse of their dark Windbreakers through the window of the rear coach. But the door had already been closed.

He raced along to the next compartment as the conductor gave the signal, and the electric express began to roll forward.

17

THE CONDUCTOR felt the door being pulled open as he tried to close it. He started to protest—it was too late to board, the train had started. But Bolan's strength was far beyond his best efforts, and the combat-ready big guy pushed his way up the steps.

The railway man scuttled away to leave the tall American by the doorway as the express gathered speed. The train accelerated south through the sooty sprawl of Tokyo's suburbs. One thing was certain: Tanaga and his friend could not escape—they were all on this train together.

Bolan sidestepped two overweight German tourists festooned with cameras. He dusted down his jacket and began to work his way along the carriage. Tanaga was in the rear coach, probably trying to devise an explanation that would not reflect too badly on himself. The assassin had to get through to report the survival of Colonel Phoenix. And Bolan intended to stop him.

The train was only half full. It was too late for those tourists who wanted to spend a full day at Umishi and too early for any business commuters. But there were some families aboard, children, innocent travelers—he could not risk starting a firefight on the train. He would settle on being close enough to keep an eye on Tanaga.

The electric "bullet" train sped through the smaller outlying depots. Two youngsters in a sports car tried to race them along the parallel highway but soon abandoned the chase. Bolan wondered how long it would take for Sandy to catch up.

He came to the last compartment. A matronly woman stopped peeling her orange to inspect the glowering foreigner.

There was a commotion at the far end, and the noise of the wind rushing outside as a door slid open. Bolan hurried through the coach. He could hear the conductor calling out in pain.

The uniformed official was sprawled on the floor at the end of the corridor. His eyes were dazed as he stared at the open door. The two thugs had smashed him to one side in their haste to get away from the approaching American.

To get away, or to lure him topside?

"No must do!" groaned the astonished conductor above the roar of the wind, struggling to sit up even as he was losing his grip on consciousness. "Must ride inside."

Bolan gave him a reassuring shrug. "Yeah, well, somebody better tell *them*."

Wrapping his fingers around the edge of the door frame, Mack Bolan backed out of the opening. The windrush buffeted him as he stretched his right foot out to reach the narrow fenderlike ledge that ran around the rear of the coach.

The next handgrip was difficult to find. His fingertips felt a ridge molded into the streamlined skin to drain away rainwater. Bolan loosened his hold on the door. The air almost blew him off as he swung around into the relative shelter of the end of the coach.

There were four indented steps provided for the maintenance crews to reach the roof. Bolan mounted them cautiously.

An overtaken motorist saw two men flattened out on the roof of the "bullet" express...and a third clambering up to join them. He very nearly collided with a streetlight.

It was impossible to stand upright on the roof. The airstream would whisk Bolan away, and he knew it. Also, the crossarms carrying the overhead cables were too low. Bolan could feel them whipping past as he crawled along the roof's service strip that went the length of the train.

Half crouching, half kneeling, he worked his way from one handgrip to the next. He managed to keep a hold on a small drainage pipe, then grasp a ventilator cowling as he advanced on the two *ninja* hit men.

"Hey, Tanaga!" Bolan yelled. "It's you and me—"

The wind filled his mouth, ballooning his cheeks. Even shouting against the airflow was impossible.

Tanaga's sidekick produced a glittering steel throwing star. He aimed at Bolan and let fly.

The razor-edged disk curved toward him, then was thrust downward by the wind. It buried itself in the roof near Bolan's hand.

The henchman gave a sharp underhand twist to the second missile. Bolan ducked as the airstream plucked the projectile up and over his head. It reached the top of its arc and clattered into one of the gridwork crossbars flashing by overhead.

Bolan drew his gun, but the weapon was as useless

in the ripping wind as the metal disks had been. It would take two men just to hold it steady—and the other guy would not cooperate if it was pointed at him. Just as Bolan reholstered the Beretta, the henchman followed Tanaga's bellowed order and launched himself toward Bolan.

He came hurtling toward the Executioner in a kamikaze attempt to drive Bolan off the roof.

Bolan stayed put, and from a crouch he supported his body with his arms as he swung out both legs in a classic scissor kick. His legs wrapped around the oncoming *ninja*'s neck, then closed in a viselike grip. The man's neck twisted, snapped.

Bolan released the wiry soldier, who slithered along the roof and vanished over the edge. The dead guy hit the stones beside the track in an explosion of bone and viscera.

Tanaga was heading for the top of the next compartment. Bolan went for him. But Tanaga was not trying to escape. He knew there was nowhere left to run. He would finish this American meddler before the same treatment was meted out to him. Bolan was still a few feet away when Tanaga turned and lashed out with a long chain he had kept concealed around his waist, under his black jacket. A deadly *ninja kasari-fundo*, the fighting chain.

The chain's weighted end wrapped itself round Bolan's forearm. Tanaga jerked hard and Bolan fell forward. His free hand shot out to grasp hold of an air duct louver. Now it was his turn to pull the chain. Maybe he could "flush" Tanaga away!

The sneering assassin held the chain taut between them for a few seconds, then kicked out at Bolan's straining fingers. Tanaga aimed to stomp loose his grip. Bolan reached forward suddenly, far enough to slacken the chain, then he tugged back hard, pulling the weapon from Tanaga's grasp.

Bolan flailed out with the chain's free end. Not to keep his enemy at bay, but to entice him.

Zeko Tanaga saw his chance. He triumphantly leaped up from his straddling position on the roof to pounce—between the lashes of the chain—in rage upon his prey.

Too late he realized the trick. He was almost upright in his crazed victory leap. The solid steel girder of the oncoming crossbar struck him at the base of his neck.

His head snapped forward, and the metal edge sliced off the back of his skull as neatly as opening a soft-boiled egg.

The terrorist made a ghastly death shudder, dribbles of gray, pink, white and red spraying around in an uneven semicircle as he jigged low along the roof.

But his mouth was still twisted in a superior sneer as the wind plucked him from the top of the coach.

Tanaga's broken body was a part of the turbulence left behind by the speeding train. One of the most dangerous terror merchants of modern times had finally been felled, the victim of a cool play by an American superagent who would not give up the chase, even when the quarry turned upon him.

Bolan disentangled himself from the chain and began to crawl back to the rear of the roof. Swinging back into the doorway was much easier than getting out.

The conductor was still massaging the huge bump on the back of his head. He stared groggily at the foreigner who came springing back in through the door.

He waited dazedly for the other two to appear. Bolan tapped him on the shoulder. "It's all right," he said. "They got off."

18

"YOU PLEASE REMAIN HERE," demanded the conductor, still totally confused by what had happened. The express was beside one of the platforms of the small Umishi terminus. "There will be some questions."

"Of course." Bolan nodded, assuring the man he would dutifully answer anything the authorities might like to ask.

As soon as the befuddled official had gone to alert the local railway policeman, Bolan let himself off the train on the side away from the platform, long-legged it across the tracks, doubled back over a pedestrian bridge and was quickly lost among the other tourists inspecting the wares outside the souvenir shops. He followed the two fat Germans aboard a sightseeing bus before the conductor and his colleague had returned to find him gone.

SO THIS WAS WHERE IT BEGAN.

The bus driver told his passengers they had one hour to wander around the shrines before going on to see Umishi's famous hot springs and mud pools.

The visitors gawked at the exquisite handiwork of the native craftsmen...while the priests pointed to the bowls where they could leave a contribution.

Bolan, his Beretta machine pistol concealed under his arm, strolled away from the crowd, circling to find the spot where the original Shinoda snapshots must have been taken.

Kenji Shinoda had visited the land of his forefathers. There was nothing unusual about that. Americans were always retracing their heritages. But, either by accident or by design, Shinoda had been in Japan at the same time as an international scientific conference. And he would have known the dates of that meeting from his professional journals.

He had driven to this peninsula and stopped to survey these peaceful shrines. And, just like the two Germans were doing, he had taken some photographs of the beautiful thatched wooden buildings. Then he had walked out to the cliff edge and snapped a few more shots of the sacred rocks below.

Shinoda had seen a small group off to the side, and a face in that group had been a familiar one from home. Akira Okawa, who headed the research and development team for Biotech Industries, looking like a solemn young owl, was in discussion with Professor Naramoto, his opposite number and potential rival at Red Sun Chemicals. Sandy had underlined that Naramoto was unmistakably marked by that odd streak of white hair. Bolan presumed that Shinoda had also recognized him.

But what of the other man? What of Kuma? If Shinoda had cared enough to make this personal pilgrimage, had he also stayed in touch enough to recognize Japan's gangster overlord? Or was the missing finger the only clue Shinoda needed to guess that Kuma was on the wrong side of the law?

Now not one of these men remained alive.

The woman, that treacherous chauffeur, was still

on the loose, but Bolan sensed she was not far away. That was good. He had a score to settle with her.

A well-behaved class of schoolchildren from Shimizu wound around the tall American, taking care not to disturb a man so deep in contemplation.

Bolan continued his thoughts. All those dead men could not have been after the secret of the brand-new biochip technology: Shinoda—the brain that could design it—had been killed first. No, there was another secret. It was enmeshed in an evil web that was spun out of Shoki Castle.

Tanaga had been but one link.

And biochemical bugs were another. Not the kind that might become the unwitting tissue of a new computer's inner workings, but a far more deadly strain—for this link stretched back through time to a bacillus bred in the festering hatreds and fervent nationalism of the prewar years, to a germ developed at a secret laboratory in Manchuria by the elder Yamazaki and his brilliant young student, Naramoto.

It was not the sea breeze stirring in the pines that caused Bolan to feel a sudden chill.

He would further wager that the power behind the Red Sun conspiracy was not interested in cryptography at all, but rather in codes of an entirely different kind, in the honor of a family name and the dreams of an empire that was never meant to be.

Bolan had seen enough. He climbed back into the bus and took a seat at the rear. Since this was an organized tour from Tokyo, there was no guide to keep a head count on the passengers. Good, then no one would miss him when he failed to ride back from the next stop.

BOLAN SMOKED A CIGARETTE before walking back to the parking area. The bus had just left without him. He waited only another five minutes before Sandy appeared.

She looked a little flustered when she got out of the car. "You got here!" Her expression registered a flicker of relief.

"Yes, I did," he replied, "but they didn't."

She looked at him with a concerned expression, then pointed at the newspaper lying on the seat beside her. She was indicating a story at the bottom of the front page.

Bolan shrugged. Those complicated little ideograms meant nothing to him. "Sorry, I can't read it."

"Neither can I, at least not all of it, but enough to make out that Kuma's been killed, and there have been two more *yakuza* executions in Osaka and Yokohama."

So the sharks were closing in for a feeding frenzy to devour Kuma's fiefdom. It sounded like the start of a full-scale gang war.

Sandy looked at him accusingly. "You knew Kuma was dead, didn't you?"

He stared past her for a few moments. Finally he nodded. "Yes, I knew."

"And tomorrow the papers will carry a story on the sudden death of poor Mr. Manutsu."

Bolan doubted if the retired wrestler was quite as poor and innocent as Sandy seemed to think. And she was certainly better off for not having heard whatever Manutsu was going to tell them.

"John, in the last twenty-four hours I've felt exhilarated and very scared." She touched his arm. "I don't want to pry into who you are or what you're doing here, but I do want to have some idea of what's going on.''

It was a fair question. In Bolan's view there was no soldier in the world who would not fight better for knowing the big picture.

"Okay, I'll tell you. I believe your story about the Circle of the Red Sun. The Circle might not be as powerful and all-pervasive as it once was, but I think the Red Sun has the most evil designs for the world. And it's headquartered at Shoki Castle."

Sandy's eyes did not leave his face.

"I don't know exactly what their plans are," he continued, "but I'll find out when I get inside the castle."

She looked enthused. Bolan shook his head. "You're not going in there."

He squatted, picked up a stick and drew a wiggly line down the left of the bare patch in front of him. "This is the coast road," he told her.

Next he scratched a lopsided oval at the bottom and to the right. "Here's where we are. The hot springs."

He waved the stick toward the fringe of trees about three hundred yards away. They could smell the sulfurous fumes of the gurgling mud pools in among the stunted pines.

"I've scouted around. I guess the castle is about a mile through those woods." He drew an X on his diagram at the point he had calculated the castle must be.

"As soon as you see me get safely through the perimeter defenses, you're to come back here for the car. The road is thickly lined with trees all the way to the main gate—there's plenty of cover—so find a good place to hide, as close to the front entrance as possible, and just wait for me."

"Lie low?"

"Yeah, very low." He glanced at his watch. "Give me until midnight. If I'm not out by then, you cut and run. And tell Paul Ryan what's happened. He'll know who else to contact."

19

BOLAN WAS A SILENT SHADOW gliding from tree to tree. Sandy could barely make him out as he signaled for her to follow. They had reached the fringe of withered foliage that lined the bank by the scalding mineral pools.

They could taste the foul air. The area had the stink of hell about it.

"Keep absolutely still," he whispered.

She froze.

Bolan did not even move his head as he scanned the thickly wooded slope on the far side.

Sandy now understood why he wanted her to move the car nearer to the castle's main entrance. It would be impossible to retrace a path across this treacherous network of slurping mud pits in the dead of night. As if to underscore the danger, a nearby fissure belched forth a cloud of superheated steam.

"He's standing right over there," said Bolan.

It took her a moment to make out the sentry half hidden in the greenery, his colorful costume acting as a camouflage in the dappled shadows beneath the trees. The man, looking away from them, remained as motionless as an Apache.

Shoki Castle was guarded by a wall of living eyes.

"He's dressed up like a samurai of the eighteenth century!" Sandy hissed in awe.

Bolan made no reply. He was timing the frequency of the geyser far to the right of their position. It bubbled up again. "Seems to go off every three minutes," he said.

To Sandy it seemed forever.

"I'm going to cross behind that geyser, using the steam cloud for cover. It will take me four to five minutes to get to the start line. The next time it blows, you work your way around to the left." His hand wheeled in the opposite direction to the one he would take.

She nodded.

Bolan did not tell Sandy to show herself occasionally through the bushes. He doubted she could crawl through the undergrowth without the guard's spotting some sign of her movement.

"I'll see you tonight." He patted her shoulder before vanishing like a dark wolf amid the twisted trees.

Bolan waited for the vent to blow its top.

It was right on time.

The breeze strung out the misty vapor into a hot white veil. Behind the fog Bolan padded swiftly over the exposed rock, the hardened mud, the scrawny grass patches. He reached the woods and paused to survey the scene to his left.

The guard was close, in profile, focused intently on the bank of scrub opposite his position. Even as Bolan began to creep toward him, the warrior drew an arrow and readied his bow. He was about to kill the woman.

Bolan took in every detail of the man's fantastic uniform. Sandy was right: this guy looked as if he'd stepped out of a samurai movie.

The sentry was taking aim when Bolan sprang from behind the nearest tree, covering yards in a single leap, and enveloped the sentry in a bear hug. Bolan reached forward with his long arms to grasp the bow and jerked back hard to wrap the weapon across the guy's windpipe. The arrow thunked harmlessly into a nearby branch.

There was a cracking sound. Not sure whether it was the bow or the man's vertebrae, Bolan kept up the relentless pressure until the sentry fell limp. With the wooden bow still bent under the guard's chin, Bolan began to drag the body toward the cover of some rocks close by. Suddenly he felt a strange drumming vibration through the ground. There was a crashing sound tearing through the bushes.

It came from the left.

And the right.

Horsemen.

"John!" Sandy's cry echoed through the forest. "John, help me!"

He raced to the border of the wood, trying to pinpoint the location of her scream.

Three mounted swordsmen were threading a zigzag path through the hot springs. They were heading for Sandy's hiding place.

Stealth was out of the question. Bolan drew the Beretta from beneath his Windbreaker and took aim.

The first 9mm hit a rider dead center at the base of the spine. He fell to the ground with a clatter of steel armaments.

The second horseman had to run his steed off the path. The crust of mineralized mud cracked beneath the horse's weight. The horse panicked as its feet broke through into churning slime.

The horseman jumped down onto solid ground. Bolan's next slug blew him back into the hole the horse had made. The guy lay at the feet of his struggling animal, his face buried in the sulfurous mud. The horse used the corpse to secure its footing, burying the sword-laden body deeper into the slime as it took off out of the steaming bog.

Bolan raced out across the same track the swordsmen had used. The third sentry was galloping to the spot where Bolan had left Sandy.

The American marksman led his running target by a hair and squeezed the trigger. The direct hit was seemingly without effect. Bolan shot once more to finally bring the sentry down.

Sandy stood up in the bushes not twenty feet from where the third horse had lost its rider. Bolan ran up the short slope and grabbed her hand. "Come on—back to the car."

"Over there, John! Behind you!"

Bolan turned to see yet another horseman, this one in bamboo armor, come storming down toward them. The rider was skillfully guiding his black mount along the safest path.

"Get going!" Bolan ordered Sandy as he took aim.

His second shot hit the rider squarely between the eyes. The impact sent his broad-brimmed war helmet flying, as an invisible force plucked the man from the saddle and tossed him back over the horse's rump.

Another rider had already reached the forest fringe.

Bolan turned and ran after the woman. In the distance he could see the wooden walkway that led back to the car park.

The bushes behind them trembled and tore as the mounted sentry came after them.

"No, not there!" Bolan shouted, reaching forward to snatch Sandy's arm to guide her to the left. "The ground's not safe."

The rider was picking his way behind them, and he was gaining.

Bolan turned to face the oncoming warrior. The man reined in and watched as the big American brought his gun to bear.

Click.

The horseman grinned at the sound. He lowered his lance into the kill position.

The sixteen-round machine pistol was not empty and Bolan knew it. He also knew the response that the faked sound of an empty gun would spark in the horseman.

He stood fast, his plan of action progressing smoothly. "Keep moving, Sandy," he shouted. "Don't stop. You've got to get back to Ryan."

But Sandy could not move. She was rooted to the spot, riveted by the sight of John Phoenix standing very still, very straight, waiting for the rider's spear-point.

The man jammed his knees into the sides of his horse; the animal responded by picking up speed, moving in fast for the kill. Bolan's muscles tensed. He was ready. The timer in his head kept pace with the animal.

When the horseman was only yards away from the Executioner, Bolan faked a quick, low move to the left. The horseman reacted by targeting the lance low and to the side. Then Bolan sprang up high.

He felt the rounded edge of the lance sweep his

rock-hard stomach as he leaped over it and grabbed the spike of death about halfway up its shaft. Landing with all his weight on it, he drove the tip of the lance into the turf. The rider was hoisted off his horse like a pole-vaulter. Bolan was left standing upright, his feet apart, with the vertical lance quivering against the side of his face.

The animal, freed from delivering death, took off into the woods. The rider lay stunned on the ground where he had fallen.

The big guy stood over the helpless man. Bolan still held his lance. Now the instrument of death was in American hands.

Looking down at the fancily decorated creep cowering under him, Bolan felt the urge to take the long lance and drive it deep into the hood's heart. But the mob soldier was defenseless. Bolan knelt, and with a quick chop of his hand, knocked the guy into a dark void.

Sandy, seeing Bolan defeat the guard, jumped into action. At last she was running for the walkway. Bolan was racing up behind her.

At the same moment they both saw four black-clad thugs angling in fast from the right. The men were sweeping around in a line that would cut the foreigners' escape route. Bolan knew they would never reach the car.

"Head for the road!" Bolan detonated. It was the only chance they had left. What had started as a silent probe was ending in a rout.

The greenery thinned out into a carefully trimmed arrangement of decorative bushes. A sloping lawn led up to the stand of pine trees that marked the highway.

Sandy prayed for traffic, another tourist bus maybe, anyone who would stop to help.

The road was directly ahead of them at the top of the rise. A car came around the bend and screeched to a halt. A man jumped out from the passenger seat and stood framed between the trees.

It was Commander Nakada.

He pulled out his gun.

Bolan looked up. The barrel was aimed right at him. Nakada fired. The bullet cleared Bolan's shoulder by inches. It raised a fountain of dirt at the bottom of the gradient, which at least slowed down the closest of the pursuers.

Nakada took a bead on the second *ninja*. Now it was clear he was shooting in order to save John Phoenix and the woman. Nakada pulled the trigger again. But again the shot was wide.

Bolan looped an arm under Sandy's shoulder and pulled her up the last few yards of the low hill that led to the road. The policeman fired a third shot, which sent the four hunters scattering for cover.

Bolan yanked open the rear door of Nakada's car. "Jump in!" Nakada fired one last round and dived into the passenger seat.

The driver gunned the car, and it took off in a cloud of grit.

"We have to get into Shoki Castle," grunted Bolan, catching his breath.

Nakada looked back at them and nodded. "That's exactly where we're going."

20

"YOU SHOULD HAVE SEEN HIM," Sandy was effusing at Nakada. "He got five or six of them! It was unbelievable...."

Bolan and Nakada locked grim glances. The commander still had not holstered his weapon.

Bolan squeezed Sandy's hand, both to silence her and to give her what little encouragement he could. "Yes, it was unbelievable. Too unbelievable. They were just herding us into a trap," he said.

Nakada turned and smiled wryly. "A trap indeed." He was pointing his Nambu 9mm handgun, unmistakable with its Browning-style frame, directly at Bolan. "And now perhaps you will hand me your gun."

The woman at the wheel glanced around briefly with a sly sneer. Bolan recognized her. He had driven down this road with her before.

"She's a lousy driver," Bolan warned Nakada as he handed over the 93-R.

"And you are a survivor, Colonel Phoenix," said the police commander.

Sandy said nothing. She was still struggling to comprehend what was happening.

"You wished to see Shoki Castle, and so you shall," said Nakada. "But you will enter it as—what should we call you?—'guests' rather than intruders."

"Release my friend here, King. She's got nothing to do with all this."

"On the contrary, Colonel, this woman has displayed an annoying curiosity about our affairs."

Sandy felt the reassuring grip of John Phoenix's hand on her own. She closed her eyes. She prayed that when she opened them this whole nightmare would be gone.

Bolan stared out the window.

This time the driver did not take the sea route detour. She turned smoothly into the castle's main entrance. A surly guard in a black Windbreaker came out of the gatehouse to inspect them. And he was being double-checked by the television camera swiveling on its mount, concealed on the overhanging branch of a chestnut tree.

The heavy wooden gateway shut behind them. They were truly prisoners now. Sandy had set out to study the past, and now she was trapped by it.

The graveled approach road wound through tranquil gardens. A slender woman in an apricot silk kimono was sitting on a stone bench beneath a paper parasol. Discreetly hovering in the background were her bodyguards. They, like all the late Tanaga's pals, were dressed in black—black combat suits.

The tree-lined avenue opened onto a broader approach area, and Bolan could see the fortress in all its grandeur.

Shoki Castle was out of an Oriental fairy tale.

It had been painstakingly restored. The playful decorative woodwork around the upper balconies contrasted with the splendid stone walls that held a promise of the mysterious and the forbidden. Two sentries in full regalia stood rigidly on either side of the main entrance. No other vehicles were in sight.

The woman at the wheel turned sharp left between two tall hedges and down a flagstoned ramp into a small underground garage. This parking area was so carefully concealed that Bolan had the impression the noble house could not confront the mechanical reality of the twentieth century. They had entered another era.

The prisoners were taken through a steel doorway and pushed along a stone passage lighted only by flickering lanterns.

"The Lord of Shoki Castle not only reveres the past," intoned Nakada as he prodded Bolan ahead of him down the dim corridor, "but he has preserved it."

They turned a corner and descended a steep flight of steps. Their footfalls echoed dully off the walls as if mocking the hopelessness of the Americans' situation. In front of them stood a stoutly barred gate.

A jailer came to meet them.

"STONE WALLS do not a prison make...." Sandy muttered the line almost to herself.

Maybe not, thought Bolan, but if so, this toad-hole was a damn good imitation. He waited for his eyes to adjust to the darkness.

The room was a plain-walled box, about twenty feet long by twelve feet wide. Bolan noted the thick iron grille that covered a ventilation duct high up on one wall. There was only one door and that was locked tight behind them.

In a moment they saw that three other prisoners occupied the cell.

One of the other prisoners got to her feet to welcome the new arrivals.

"Hello, Suki," Bolan said. She reached out with her hand, but the big man gave her a brief hug instead. "Sandy, I'd like you to meet Setsuko Seki."

The two women shook hands in the formal Western manner.

"You were supposed to be ill," Sandy said.

"Ill? I was drugged, then tossed in here. I work for my country's internal security service. We police the police, as it were." Suki held up her thumb and finger about an inch apart. "I was this close to building the case against Nakada," she said to Bolan, "but Nakada struck first." Suki shrugged. "Colonel, Sandy, this gentleman is Professor Naramoto, and this is his wife, Kiko."

The lady got up and bowed. Her husband remained slumped against the wall, but even in the candlelight the streak of white hair clearly identified him as the missing scientist. Sandy sat down next to him and gently patted his hand.

"I think his mind is going," Suki uttered under her breath.

Bolan steered Suki to the far end of the cell so they could continue alone in low whispers. "What's going on here?" Bolan asked.

"For months I was investigating possible charges against Kingoro Nakada. We knew about his connections with the Kuma-*kumi*, but the more I uncovered, the more it pointed to a deeper conspiracy—something that involved Red Sun."

"How did they get their hooks into the King of the City?"

"Nakada was one of them from the very start. He was groomed to attend the police academy and then work his way up from within. Powerful friends, inside and out, helped insure his rapid promotion.''

"He knew the professor was being kept here all the time.''

"Yes. As far as I can make out, the professor was working on a top-secret project. But perhaps you know more about that than I do, Colonel. The one time he spoke in here, he said, 'But I was working for them. I was working for the Americans.' Does that make sense to you?''

Bolan shook his head.

BOLAN WAS GIVEN the imperial treatment.

Four guards.

Two in front and two behind.

His hands were bound together behind his back with wire.

He felt very much a Very Important Prisoner. The terror goons were taking him up into the interior of the castle. Just Bolan, not the others. In the close confines of the corridors, even the silken rustle of the guards' traditional costumes and the soft pad of their slippers seemed loud. Each man wore a long sword and a short sword tucked into his sash.

Yamazaki certainly had retreated from modern civilization—and, mused Bolan, perhaps from his sanity—to have recreated this lost world of samurai, *ninja*, and almond-eyed courtesans.

Someone was going to have to bring him back to reality.

Bolan noticed that the back of each guard's sash was decorated with a chrysanthemum embroidered in gold thread. The master of Shoki Castle was ambitious indeed, for Bolan understood the symbol of that bloom to be reserved only for the Emperor himself.

So the trip back to reality would be a long one.

Which was fine by the Executioner. He could stay the course. . . .

They reached an underground T-junction. The passage to the left was barred by a thick steel door marked with a stenciled skull and crossbones. Bolan did not have to read Japanese to recognize Keep Out. The guard forced Bolan to the right.

The area they had reached was better lit than the bowels of the castle. It appeared to be the guards' quarters. Humid air rushed into the corridor when a figure opened a door to the side. That must be the bathhouse. A bronzed retainer emerged, wearing nothing but a towel, and he lounged in the doorway to sneer at the rangy foreigner being led past. One of the guards stopped to share a joke with him.

Bolan was taken up another broader flight of steps.

All the way he had mentally mapped the layout of the castle.

Now he was pushed through a curtained entrance and into the main hall.

A large man, with a notched scar in his brow that pointed down to one milky eye, accepted delivery of the bound prisoner. The four guards fell to their knees and bowed toward the raised dais. Their foreheads touched the ground.

Bolan looked at the slender, imposing figure sitting cross-legged before him on a plump cushion.

Suddenly One Eye moved behind him and unleashed a savage blow to his kidneys. "Kneel before the Lord of the Red Sun!"

21

Bolan staggered forward but kept on his feet. "I won't bow to any man," he said through gritted teeth. "Least of all to you, Yamazaki."

The middle-aged man on the dais waved One Eye away. For now, the warlord would exact no punishment for such insolence. He had a special fate in mind for this remarkable American.

Hideo Yamazaki had a triangular face and a neat black mustache, but it was his eyes and their glittering hardness that caught Bolan's attention.

In front of him were two thin cushions. On one lay the silenced Beretta. From the other, Yamazaki picked up two short strips of film. "You have been searching for these negatives, I believe."

"I've been looking for the reason that a man was killed for taking those photographs."

"More than one man has been killed." The tone of the Japanese mob warlord's voice was gently chiding, but his eyes accused Bolan directly and fiercely. Then Yamazaki turned his head slightly to the side to look at Nakada, who was listening from the shadows.

"The police have been such useful associates," Yamazaki hissed.

Bolan glanced across at Nakada, intending to drive even the slightest wedge between him and his master.

"But like all your associates," the nightscorcher said, "they are disposable."

"I decide when a person has expended his usefulness," spat Yamazaki. He spoke English like a mean cop. To control the conversation, Yamazaki drew attention to the Beretta by bending over to examine it as if it were something from the future. Then he pushed the flat cushion away in disdain. A servant stepped forward with a white cloth to wipe off the slightest trace of gun oil from the *daimyo*'s slender fingers. The mob overlord addressed One Eye abruptly. "Remove the weapon."

The retainer bowed low as he retreated, bearing off the handgun.

"Kuma...Zeko Tanaga...my magnificent horsemen..." recited Yamazaki. "You have been very busy, Colonel Phoenix."

"And you're full of it, Yamazaki."

"On the contrary, I remain undefiled by anything but the purest revenge." The steel in the Japanese gangster's voice was unmistakable. "Perhaps I am different from you, for I am devoted to revenge. And I have waited too long for it. I shall have my revenge, Colonel. Nobody—least of all you—will be able to stop me."

"Revenge for your father—is that what you're after, revenge for the execution of Colonel Yamazaki?"

"It is the vengeance of the Jonin," nodded the *daimyo*, "for the line continues."

"The *lie* continues."

Yamazaki signaled angrily for Bolan to hold his tongue.

"How can you absolve your father?" persisted the big guy.

"My father was banished, Colonel Phoenix, sent to the wilds of Manchuria." The Japanese *capo*'s eyes dimmed as he reflected on the injustice of the past. "But he continued with his work and developed the most potent bacteriological weapons ever devised."

So Sandy was right.

"Japan need never have surrendered. The Allied forces could have been destroyed, pushed back clear across the Pacific. My father was a genius, Colonel Phoenix."

"You had no chance to know your father, Yamazaki. He was a war criminal."

The feudal dreamer ignored Bolan's charge, just as he had ignored the facts all his life. Objective reality would not be allowed to intrude—especially now that he had all the power and the weapons to kill and torture and oppress innocent people, regardless of reality.

"A genius, yes, but I have surpassed even his achievements. It has taken many years, but I have perfected a new gas gangrene strain, Anthrax-B and Diogene."

"*You* perfected it? Or did Professor Naramoto?"

"He was of great assistance to me," conceded Yamazaki. "It would be a pity if he should not see these long years of effort bear fruit."

"And all this time you made him believe he was working for the U.S."

"Perhaps that's what he wanted to believe, Colonel. In the years following the war he was grateful for the refuge offered him by the Red Sun Corporation.

Fear is the surest jailer. When I became interested in continuing my father's work, it was not difficult to persuade the professor that he was secretly working for the Americans.''

Mack Bolan knew this kind of creature who sat before him. Animal Man. But this time there was a difference. The creatures of the Mob, or the terrorists who were so callously indifferent to the pain and misery that they inflicted, would always try to justify themselves, raving their rancid hatreds and twisted ambitions, but where they were crude and ranting, this man was composed, refined. That unpleasant difference only made Yamazaki all the more chilling.

"Did you not pass yourself off to Commander Nakada as a security expert visiting Japan to inspect our latest techniques in that field? When in fact you intended to penetrate the secret of the Circle of the Red Sun?"

"I was investigating the death of Kenji Shinoda.''

"Ah, yes. Shinoda. He was—I believe you have an expression—'a fly in the ointment'? Well, he was a troublesome fly that had to be squashed.''

"You make me puke.''

Bolan heard a quick footstep behind him and braced for the blow. One Eye had returned and was now intent on striking down the *gaijin* for his brazenness.

"Let me talk with him!" screamed Yamazaki, waving the henchman back. He stared at Bolan with an intensity that made the mobster seem youthful, yet possessed, mad.

"I needed someone to whom we could dispatch the A-B and Diogene germs, somebody above suspicion," he continued. "He had to be a man who knew how to *disperse* them properly. Okawa was perfect for my plans. But then Shinoda tried to blackmail Okawa into working on a computer project. Therefore I eliminated him for his interference.''

"At least Okawa had the decency to do away with himself when he realized what he was involved in,'' growled Bolan.

"As you have said, they were all disposable. The only thing that matters has been my plan. I shall now use the network established by Tanaga to smuggle those vials into the United States.''

Pointing arrogantly with a gloved hand, Yamazaki indicated two small glass cases that sat on a bench behind him, each filled with a number of little sealed bottles of colorless liquid. "These are phonies, of course. I have them to impress you. The genuine ones are in the laboratory here in my castle. I would not like to be too close to them! Mix their contents with a special nutrient base, and enough bacteria will breed overnight to wipe out the west coast of your country. The attack will be centered on San Diego, Los Angeles and San Francisco,'' he crowed. "Now you Americans can taste defeat.''

Yamazaki waited for a response, but Mack Bolan denied him the pleasure.

"All that remains is to test our product on human subjects,'' said Yamazaki calmly. "Tomorrow morning we shall begin with the women. Your women. You can watch! And then it will be your turn.''

Still Bolan betrayed no reaction.

"Take him away! And keep him isolated from the others. Until tomorrow then, Colonel.''

The bound American spoke at last. "Nuts,'' he said.

22

So it had come to this. From a dark, deserted street in Los Angeles to a dungeon deep beneath a medieval fortress in Japan, Mack Bolan had followed a descent into murderous hell.

Yamazaki was a madman, that was for sure. In Mack Bolan's opinion he was an archetypal agent of chaos.

The Yamazaki family line had reached a nadir of world-threatening evil. It was time to cut the line off.

And Bolan would be the sword.

Mack Bolan's job was to survive and to endure. The Executioner had been a warrior all his adult life. Indeed he had become the most effective single-man fighting force in the history of world combat, and endure he damned well would.

Something sword-sharp and brilliant had happened to Bolan in his transformation to Colonel John Phoenix. His power to control the outcome of combat had increased in direct proportion to the sickening growth of fanaticism around the world.

It was almost as if he grew stronger from the sheer horror of his foes. Colonel Phoenix had become a new kind of Mack Bolan, a Bolan who was revived by his never-ending attrition of the world's enemies. He came to life—big life, lived large—whenever the threat became unmanageable by any other force than

Stony Man's. The terror implicit in today's world was Colonel Phoenix's lifeblood. It made him a giant among men as never before. A giant who was cool, collected, always prepared, fearsomely ready: a big calm guy who took the first shot.

John Phoenix was a warrior who dispatched the enemy and disappeared even before bystanders had turned to look.

Mack Bolan—Stony Man's magnificent number one—identified the psychopathic terrormongers and he did something about them to make good men sleep securely once more.

Bolan turned to inspect the cell. It was much like the other holding room, only smaller. The walls were as bare, and once again the place was dark. Above the door, vaguely visible, were about half a dozen pipes of varying diameters. Judging from the cell's location at the farthest end of a corridor, these metal tubes must either serve the lab or the bathhouse on the floor above.

The tubes were just beyond the reach of his outstretched hand. Bolan jumped several times and touched each of them. One was hot, two lukewarm, and the others were cold. And they were all attached very firmly to the wall.

He crouched in the corner, recharging his energy, drawing on hidden strengths within, searching for a weakness without as he retraced the layout of the castle in his mind.

If Colonel Yamazaki had been banished, then executed, what had happened to the other seven of the Jonin clique? Perhaps that is what Manutsu had intended to tell him—that the legendary Jonin had no power left except through Hideo Yamazaki.

No doubt his lordship intended to resurrect the Jonin Circle, presumably in his own image, once he had struck his first terrible blow. Tanaga's pipeline into California was efficient enough to transport the deadly vials. The guy had smuggled himself in and out successfully. Two small containers should prove no problem, even if he was no longer alive to escort them.

There was a sound at the doorway. Bolan glanced up to see the toadlike guard back on duty already, peering in through the small barred opening on the door. The creep was taking a personal delight in the fate of the brawny foreigner locked up in solitary confinement.

The guards evidently were not going to check on him as frequently as they had in the earlier cell; confident that he was not going anywhere, they only peered in through the small window every four or five minutes.

Bolan wondered where in the castle grounds their training center was, and if it held a modern armory.

He was also intrigued at what part hypnosis—*saimin-jutsu*, as Yumoto had called it—played in their preparation. Tanaga had undoubtedly been reprogrammed from the volatile enthusiasm of his terrorist days into a *ninja* assassin by some kind of mind-control system. Bolan could recall the black burning coals that were Tanaga's eyes. Yamazaki's eyes glittered with the same fire of self-righteous madness.

It must be put out.

Once and for all.

Bolan heard the low buzz of conversation in the passageway. He crept to the door and sneaked a look through the bars.

One Eye had come down to check on the guard detail personally. He was showing Toad Face the American's gun. Evidently he had not got rid of it as ordered—he was keeping the Beretta as a trophy. The two men chuckled over the prospect of using their prisoners as live subjects for Lord Yamazaki's experiments, as One Eye loaded the weapon, probably with cheap copycat 9mm slugs, and tucked the automatic into his sash.

Bolan had no doubt that in a few moments the man with the milky eye would appear at the window to gloat. Maybe it was time to wipe that smile off his scarred face. Time to tear a leaf from the *ninja*'s own book of tricks.

Bolan stood directly under the pipes, jumped and caught a firm hold and swung himself up in one fluid movement. He twisted around to lie horizontal between the pipes, with his arms and legs hooked over the metal casings to maintain his precarious balance.

In less than a minute he heard someone lean against the door to check on him. There was a sharp hiss of indrawn breath as the jailer stared in dismay at the empty cell.

The key rattled in the lock, and the door was thrown open. One Eye marched in. Toad Face was right on his heels.

One Eye sensed the danger from above. He was instinctively drawing his sword and turning as Bolan dropped on top of the pudgy guard behind. They went down in a heap. One Eye's weapon was clear of its scabbard, and he wasted no time in swinging the blade.

Bolan heaved the befuddled Toad Face around, using his fat body to block the other man's blow. The steel edge of the samurai *katana* sword sliced through the fat one's collarbone, slashing deep into his chest cavity. Toad Face's eyes popped wide open with the double shock that he was dead, and that he had been killed by his own superior officer.

One Eye tried to drag his sword free from the corpse. In that split second, Bolan grabbed the front of the hardguy's robe and pulled him off balance. As One Eye fell forward, his face met Bolan's forehead coming up—hard.

One Eye dropped on his ass, seeing stars. The Executioner was not in a forgiving mood. He ripped out the dead Toad Face's sword and rammed it under One Eye's ribs.

Both of the Japanese retainers were now leaking sticky red puddles on the flagstones.

Bolan put his foot against One Eye's chest and tugged out the sword. He removed Toad Face's belt, with its two *shaken* stars hooked on it.

The *shaken* throwing stars were palm-sized, made of flat steel and were the color and texture of circular saw blades. They might come in very useful.

Bolan then stripped Toad Face of his torn black woolen shirt. He removed his own dirt-caked denim shirt and put on the collarless black *ninja* garment. Although it had been worn by a much bulkier individual, its material fitted him tightly. With his own black pants, Bolan now looked like a *ninja* himself, except for a black mask.

He felt comfortable complementing the several black-suited *ninja* he was about to do battle with. He would be even more comfortable with one more important item.

In the doorway lay the Beretta where it had fallen

in the fray. Bolan retrieved the compact weapon, though there was no sign of its special elongated holster. The full-automatic piece felt uncommonly light in his hand compared with the AutoMag he'd left in the States. Holster or not, he was now back in business.

He strapped on the belt and tucked the gun into the right-hand side. Then he hoisted one of the *katana* swords and plunged that into his belt, too. It was grim attire once more, but it made Bolan feel alive.

The regiment that protected this evil place seemed divided in two: the colorfully costumed sentries were the regular household retainers, no doubt as deadly as they were decorative, while the smaller detachment of black-clad *ninja* were headquartered here between bloody missions beyond the castle walls. And, out on the streets, Yamazaki had been able to call on another army of muscle: Kuma's gang. Every one of them was willing to sacrifice his life for the self-styled Lord of the Red Sun.

It was little wonder that no one had ever penetrated this forbidden circle and lived to tell the tale.

He heard someone running to investigate. The second jailer, Toad Face's companion, raced in through the open doorway. He was stopped dead in his tracks, literally. Bolan put such force behind his blow at the speeding man's face that he broke the guy's neck.

Bolan seized the bunch of keys from the gurgling corpse, then checked the corridor outside. It was empty. He would have to move fast. He hurried to the far end of the corridor to free the others.

Suki did not seem surprised to see him. She had

observed the colonel in action and was confident he would get the better of the guards.

Bolan spoke to Sandy. "You remember the way back to the garage?"

"Yes—I think so."

"Give Mrs. Naramoto a hand with the professor. Easy now. . .it isn't far. Suki, you and I bring up the rear."

The scientist nodded at Bolan as he clambered uncertainly to his feet. For the first time he seemed confident that he understood what was going on. "I told you so," he said to his wife as Suki translated. "It's the Americans. I knew they'd come."

The four fugitives made painfully slow progress up the first flight of stairs. They could only go at the pace of the professor, who found the steep stone steps a tiring climb.

"I'll have to leave you at the next landing," Bolan whispered to Suki. "Look after the others."

She nodded, accepting the responsibility.

"See if you can hot-wire Nakada's car. If not, you'll have to make a break for it on foot. Get well clear of the castle, okay?"

Again Suki nodded. She knew the colonel had a score to settle. And she knew that nothing was going to stop him.

Bolan slipped away from them.

Suddenly the door at the side of the passageway opened. Through it stepped Nakada and his evil female driver. "Phoenix—"

Suki spun around at the sound of Nakada's startled cry.

"Get away!" Bolan ordered the startled Sandy. One or other of them had to get out to warn Paul

Ryan. But Sandy froze. Suki ran back toward Bolan.

Nakada had no time for the quaint courtesies of samurai combat—he attacked Bolan like a savage warrior.

Suki ran straight past Bolan, launched herself and landed feet first in the driver's ribs.

Nakada's fingers hooked for a lethal attack. His arm flew forward like a snake striking. Bolan sidestepped, seized Nakada's wrist and swung him into the wall. He had twisted so savagely that Nakada's shoulder separated.

The female driver never recovered from Suki's first assault. She tried to catch her breath, but Suki's knuckles dug deep into her solar plexus. The woman struggled to avoid the rigid edge of Suki's hand that smashed down across her throat. She failed, fell and cracked her head against the floor.

Bolan stole one quick glance at Suki: she was taking care of business without his help.

Nakada cursed and, despite one arm dangling uselessly from its socket, aimed a kick at Bolan's groin. Bolan's hand cupped behind Nakada's ankle and he flipped him backward. Nakada hit the cold flagstones hard. He was out for the count.

The driver was struggling to her feet. Suki delivered another punishing chop that drove her back to her knees. Before Bolan could stop her, the young policewoman felled the driver with a blow that would have dropped an ox.

Suki frisked the unconscious body and produced the car keys. Then she pulled the Luger from the driver's shoulder holster and silently offered it to Bolan. He patted the Beretta tucked in his belt and shook his head. "No, you take it. Now get out of here, all of you!"

Sandy was still standing awe-struck. She was feeling a chill deep inside. In the flickering lamplight she saw John Phoenix only as a tall warrior in black, gun and sword thrust into his belt, and he looked like the deadliest *ninja* that had ever lived.

"Okay, let's go," ordered Suki. "Good luck, Colonel."

Bolan watched them retreat down the dimly lighted tunnel toward the garage. The professor was still trying to explain his garbled delusions to his wife. Bolan was not too concerned. Suki would watch out for them.

He moved quickly back in the direction of the guards' quarters. There was no time to look for a safe way through the maze of underground passages that riddled the rocks beneath Shoki Castle. He was making directly for the laboratory where he knew the original vials were kept, even if it meant fighting all the way through hell to get there.

23

FROM BEHIND A DOOR came the muffled sound of tipsy laughter and the sharper clink of a bottle. Bolan shrank back in the shadows. The door handle rattled. A shaft of smoky light spilled out and a man emerged.

Bolan ducked farther back into the nearest available entrance. There was nowhere else to conceal himself. The small cubicle he had stepped into was a double doorway designed to keep moist warm air in the bathhouse. The silenced machine pistol in hand, he eased open the inner door.

He had his bearings now. There should be an exit on the far side of the baths. Bolan peered into the large clammy room.

A row of showers was arranged along one side for bathers to wash themselves before immersing their bodies in sunken cedar-lined tubs. The steaming pools were large and rectangular, and the water's surface was almost flush with the tiled floor.

Only one man was actually enjoying a late-night soak in the tubs. Bolan walked boldly into the bathhouse.

The solitary bather gripped the edge of the cedar planking and rose to protest the intrusion of a fully dressed man.

Simultaneously a gong reverberated through the

halls outside. Someone, somewhere, had tripped over a body. The alarm was being sounded.

He had to work fast now.

The far door opened and one of the *ninja* gang ran in. Bolan shot him before he had taken three paces. The *ninja* fell on the tiles and slithered upside down to the very edge of a pool. His head and shoulders fell back into the water. The jets in the cedarwood underneath the surface started spouting red-stained water around the head. It must have been a head.

Bolan took cover when a second black-attired bodyguard appeared. The newcomer looked incredulously at his fallen comrade. The original bather was already fleeing the bathhouse.

"Your friend's taking a drink," explained Bolan to the *ninja*. "Care to join him?"

Chest hit. Dead center.

The man staggered and toppled sideways into the mist-enshrouded pool. Bolan ran past him for the open door.

Half a dozen of Yamazaki's men were racing off toward the cells. He watched the last of them turn at the far end of the corridor, then Bolan ran the other way.

He found a guard on duty outside a locked door with the sign of the grinning skull on it. The guard was visibly troubled by the clanging of the alarm.

Trouble exploded in his face. In the form of The Executioner.

Bolan fired twice at very short range. The first shot blew the sentry back against the wall. The second shot was just to stop his squirming.

Bolan spun a wheel on the door and tugged open the heavy metal access. There was a shout behind him. From within the doorway, Bolan snapped off one more shot. The bullet tore through the leading onrusher's throat, then the mangled metal slug cartwheeled into the face of the man behind. By then, Bolan was slamming the door.

He found a length of piping to wedge into the wheel lock on the inside of the door.

Crazed men hammered on the outside. Bolan turned to view a small changing room with lockers and benches, and beyond, visible through a window in a far door, the glaringly lighted laboratory—the innermost secret of Shoki Castle.

He guessed the small antechamber to be a decontamination room. He would not be able to proceed without fulfilling certain protective procedures. He pulled a white suit from a row of protective suits, gloves and helmets that were lined up on hooks.

Bolan took off his belt and put aside his gun and sword, then stepped swiftly into the one-piece asbestos garment and pulled it up over his shoulders. He grabbed a helmet made of ceramic and metal with a clear glass visor and a breathing filter at chin level and secured it in place over his head. Gloves next, tucked tight under the sleeve fastenings. Then he retrieved his sword.

He reached for the door to the laboratory. As he touched the door latch, fluorescent tubes above him began to glow. Before the door lock was automatically released, the radiation tubes built in intensity until they discharged a single blinding flash, leaving Bolan bathed in an eerie afterglow.

The enforced sterilization procedure was complete, and the door responded to Bolan's push.

Behind him, screams of rage at the shored-up outer

door receded as the door of the antechamber clicked shut. Before him, everything was white—walls, floors, ceilings, storage spaces, doors.

In a split second, the nightfighter absorbed the chilling scene. Long benches were laden with glass retorts, coiled transparent tubing, flasks full of bubbling mixtures, dishes of bilious colored cultures, electrical wiring and a thousand instruments to test, control and record the results of Yamazaki's experiments.

On the far wall above a tangled mass of equipment was mounted a polished wooden panel that held a huge ceremonial sword, its long blade positioned vertical to the ground. There was a Japanese inscription engraved in the wood beneath the sharp tip of the sword. Bolan decided the weapon was some ghoulish memento of Hideo's family history. It stood as a symbol of power and vicious intent in this sterile chamber, where the biochemical conspiracies of a death cult were hatched in oozing test tubes.

In his helmet and asbestos suit, Bolan strode down the broad passageway between the lab benches. He would wreck as much of the equipment as he could before the doors behind him were broken apart by his pursuers. At the top of the list were the two cases of germ vials that would look like the glass cases the foul Hideo had shown off to him in his throne room. He sought them out, found them.

They were placed on a table on either side of a large straw-packed vessel full of acid. Bolan pushed the vessel over with his foot and let the contents slurp out onto the floor into a small lake, while he used the sword to pry open the first glass case of deadly virus.

Three bottles containing volatile spirits were sitting

on the edge of the same table. Bolan swept them off with the flat of his sword. They shattered on impact and the different chemicals formed a larger, oily, smoking puddle. The suit protected him from the noxious fumes, but Bolan was careful where he trod as he next upended the first glass container of deadly germs. The small glass bulbs tumbled out, hissing as they hit the floor and cracked open.

Bolan turned to the second chest of bacteria. Its contents, too, joined the now vividly colored slime that coated the tiles. The smorgasbord of elements that was splashed across the floor would, Bolan hoped, help mute the power of the dangerous bacteria by exposing them to acidic deterioration. A small-scale but total germ war was going on right at his feet. Anthrax and gangrene and their nutrient base raged to survive in the hostile environment of acid and other brimstones from hell.

Bolan heard harsh rasping for breath through his headset.

He spun around.

Yamazaki stood at a concealed private entranceway, attired in an anti-contamination suit and helmet, surveying the boiling wreckage of his life's work.

"You fool—you cannot destroy an idea!" The voice echoed in Bolan's helmet. "I have perfected these strains. You cannot eradicate that knowledge!"

"No, *you* didn't perfect them," said Bolan. "It was the work of Naramoto."

"That's not true—"

"And now he'd rather destroy his own mind than let you unlock its secrets with hypnosis!"

Bolan raised his sword in a two-handed hold above his head.

The Lord of the Red Sun would not refuse this final challenge.

Hideo would insure that this was to be a duel without parallel.

There would be no need for a deep thrust. No major artery need be severed. The merest scratch, a single cut through the fabric of their protective suits would insure an agonizing death. The lab was awash with some of the deadliest bacteria ever mutated.

The two warriors stood facing each other squarely, dressed from head to foot like astronauts about to stand on the moon, yet each man bore a *katana* blade hand-forged in an earlier century.

The eyes of Yamazaki burned through his visor with an implacable hatred as he took up the opening stance.

Even Tanaga himself must have been mesmerized by those glittering slits, thought Bolan. Kuma, too. And Nakada. They had bent before Yamazaki's will. They had sold their souls to be admitted to his secret circle.

"You sacrifice yourself for no purpose," said Yamazaki. His tone was now almost cordial. "You are one of us, Colonel...."

Inviting.

"An outsider."

Quietly convincing.

"An outcast...yet a warrior."

Perceptive.

"A wandering samurai. You are *ronin*."

Sympathetic.

"You dress as we do, think as we do, act as we do...."

Confident now.

"They gave you a rank, but you are your own man."

Truthful.

"You are the masterless *ninja*."

Flattering.

"This is your place. Here!"

Demanding....

"No!" It was a struggle for Bolan to issue even that simple, hoarse denial. He had been listening to the words, almost seduced by the tone, watching those eyes...and now Yamazaki was nearly upon him.

He had not seen the other man move—he would swear to that—but somehow Yamazaki had approached close enough to strike. It seemed as if he had glided across the floor.

Bolan managed to raise his weapon and parry the blow. The hypnotic spell was shattered as sparks flew from the clashing steel.

"No, I am not one of you!" It was Bolan's turn to press home the attack. Yamazaki fell back before the angry flurry of flashing strokes, the razor-sharp edges scraping, chipping, clanging against each other.

Hideo was driven back to his starting point.

Bolan poised for the first and final cut. He was beyond thought, unimpeded by careful plans—mind dissolved into instinct—as the sword thrust itself forward like a live thing in his hands.

He felt his foot slipping in the fizzing sludge.

Yamazaki's savage counterstroke deflected his

blade. It slapped flat down on the surface of the workbench. A second chop cleaved the ancient steel apart, leaving Bolan holding only the broken hilt.

He dodged backward quickly to get beyond range of Yamazaki's sword point.

But Yamazaki was in no hurry. The American officer was defenseless. Now he could dispose of his adversary slowly, painfully, remorsefully, here beneath the wall-mounted sword of his father. How symbolic.

"You should have listened," said the Lord of Shoki Castle. His mocking laughter boomed in the *gaijin*'s ears.

"I could not," said Bolan, lifting back his arm, "for I am your executioner!"

He threw the heavy broken handle over Yamazaki's head. It hit the wooden display board hard... the sword trembled, slipped from its pegs and plunged downward.

It slit the suit between Yamazaki's shoulder blades before clattering to the floor. Yamazaki was unaware of the puncture, but almost immediately the point of his weapon started wavering in an uncertain circle.

One leg collapsed beneath him. Yamazaki reached out, trying to steady himself, and knocked several more bottles flying as his arm swept over the work top.

Yamazaki crumpled to his knees. The air rushing into his suit was killing him. He began to choke.

Bolan picked up a bottle of inflammable spirits and began stuffing a torn rag into its neck.

"Colonel!" Yamazaki held out one hand in an imploring gesture. He was begging to be finished off quickly.

Bolan reached out with his foot and shoved the long sword back toward Yamazaki before walking to the decon chamber. As he closed the airlock, Bolan took one last look to see Yamazaki slowly push the steel point into his lower abdomen, starting at the left and then slicing across to the right.

Then he left the Lord of the Red Sun committing hara-kiri in the solitary shambles of his own nightmare.

24

THE MEN CROWDED outside the lab's changing area were eagerly waiting for their master to emerge triumphant. The decon hatch swung back on its hinges, and they were served a Molotov cocktail. Three men tumbled backward, their clothes afire; four more were so deprived of oxygen in the conflagration that they collapsed where they were.

Bolan, in black again with his belt back on, hurried through the bitter smoke. Now he resorted to the *shaken*. One soldier running down the corridor did not have the sense to drop the water buckets he was carrying before a three-pointed star buried itself in his forehead.

The alarm gong was sounding with a renewed frenzy. *Fire!*

As he strode along the passage, Bolan knocked over every lantern he could find, each new blaze adding its own heat to the inferno that roared through the chambers and crevices of Shoki Castle. Bolan's rage cut through the rolling clouds that were smothering everything else in confusion.

The stairs were ahead of him.

The steps to freedom. . .and clean, fresh air.

"COLONEL PHOENIX! OVER HERE!"

They were waiting for him in the darkness, in the

shelter of a tall hedge. Suki, Sandy, Professor Naramoto and his wife.

When Bolan reached them, the professor was staring up at the smoke-smudged stars. His mind was back in 1945, lost forever in the fires of history. His wife wept.

"John, I never thought I'd see you again," murmured Sandy, coming to the side of the black-clad terrorscourger and holding him tight around the waist.

"You should have more faith," smiled Suki knowingly. She was well aware of the American colonel's high aims and strengths to match, being of the same inclination herself. She looked him in the eye, and the look lingered. This was the man who had set the fires from which they now sheltered. This was one true blitzer.

"I have a report to make," Bolan grunted. He led the way to the nearby Datsun, its engine running.

He was impatient to make contact with Hal Brognola to wrap up the latest episode in his endless new war.

He was impatient to make contact with April Rose, too. For that, he would have to return to the States. It was an arousing thought.

Once more he turned to watch the tongues of flame that blossomed from the castle windows. Tendrils of blue white fire ran across the wooden tiles to the upturned curves of the roof corners.

Yamazaki's mad dream was going up in smoke.

Consumed by fire.

The cleansing fire.

The purifying fire of justice.

MACK
BOLAN

THE EXECUTIONER 54

appears again in
Mountain Rampage

A viperous organization coiled within the crannies of the Colorado Rockies has created a drug that causes mind surrender, then death. The entire United States is in peril of becoming a terminal rest home.

Mack Bolan's nightfighting mandate: penetrate the highly guarded compound, destroy the fortress and snuff out the mountainside maniacs. Fast.

Coming soon:

MACK BOLAN FIGHTS ALONGSIDE
ABLE TEAM AND PHOENIX FORCE
in

STONY MAN DOCTRINE

Beyond Law . . . Beyond Sanction!

This thrilling mega-novel has changed in concept and
development since our last announcement. To keep
pace with events in today's world, Mack Bolan's
greatest adventure has grown even bigger!

America stands alone against the most powerful
military regime in history. In four days of horror,
Mack Bolan and his Stony Man people are forced to
exceed the authority of the President himself, just as
Bolan has always fought above and beyond the law—
because justice and survival are at stake!

"Understand this, all of you. This is the big one. This
is 'dirty war.' No surrender!"

—*Mack Bolan*

**GOLD
EAGLE**

Available soon wherever paperbacks are sold.

MACK BOLAN

THE EXECUTIONER SERIES

I am not their judge. I am their judgment—I am their executioner.
— *Mack Bolan,*
a.k.a. Col. John Phoenix

Mack Bolan is the free world's leading force in the new Terrorist Wars, defying all terrorists and destroying them piece by piece, using his Vietnam-trained tactics and knowledge of jungle warfare. Bolan's new war is the most exciting series ever to explode into print. You won't want to miss a single word. Start your collection now!

GOLD EAGLE

Available wherever paperbacks are sold.

Mack Bolan's

PHOENIX FORCE

AN EXECUTIONER SERIES

by Gar Wilson

Phoenix Force is The Executioner's five-man army that blazes through the dirtiest of encounters. Like commandos who fight for the love of battle and the righteous unfolding of the logic of war, Bolan's five hardasses make mincemeat out of their enemies. Catch up on the whole series now!

"Strong-willed and true. Gold Eagle Books are making history. Full of adventure, daring and action!"

—*Marketing Bestsellers*

#1 **Argentine Deadline** #4 **Tigers of Justice**
#2 **Guerilla Games** #5 **The Fury Bombs**
#3 **Atlantic Scramble**

Phoenix Force titles are available wherever paperbacks are sold.

GOLD EAGLE

HE'S EXPLOSIVE.
HE'S UNSTOPPABLE.
HE'S MACK BOLAN!

He learned his deadly skills in Vietnam…then put them to use by destroying the Mafia in a blazing one-man war. Now **Mack Bolan** is back to battle new threats to freedom, the enemies of justice and democracy—and he's recruited some high-powered combat teams to help. **Able Team**—Bolan's famous Death Squad, now reborn to tackle urban savagery too vicious for regular law enforcement. And **Phoenix Force**—five extraordinary warriors handpicked by Bolan to fight the dirtiest of anti-terrorist wars around the world.

Fight alongside these three courageous forces for freedom in all-new, pulse-pounding action-adventure novels! Travel to the jungles of South America, the scorching sands of the Sahara and the desolate mountains of Turkey. And feel the pressure and excitement building page after page, with nonstop action that keeps you enthralled until the explosive conclusion! Yes, Mack Bolan and his combat teams are living large…and they'll fight against all odds to protect our way of life!

Now you can have all the new Executioner novels delivered right to your home!

You won't want to miss a single one of these exciting new action-adventures. And you don't have to! Just fill out and mail the coupon following and we'll enter your name in the Executioner home subscription plan. You'll then receive four brand-new action-packed books in the Executioner series every other month, delivered right to your home! You'll get two **Mack Bolan** novels, one **Able Team** and one **Phoenix Force**. No need to worry about sellouts at the bookstore…you'll receive the latest books by mail as soon as they come off the presses. That's four enthralling action novels every other month, featuring all three of the exciting series included in The Executioner library. Mail the card today to start your adventure.

FREE! Mack Bolan bumper sticker.

When we receive your card we'll send your four explosive Executioner novels and, absolutely FREE, a Mack Bolan "Live Large" bumper sticker! This large, colorful bumper sticker will look great on your car, your bulletin board, or anywhere else you want people to know that you like to "Live Large." And you are under no obligation to buy anything—because your first four books come on a 10-day free trial! If you're not thrilled with these four exciting books, just return them to us and you'll owe nothing. The bumper sticker is yours to keep, FREE!

Don't miss a single one of these thrilling novels…mail the card now, while you're thinking about it. And get the Mack Bolan bumper sticker FREE!

BOLAN FIGHTS AGAINST ALL ODDS TO DEFEND FREEDOM!

Mail this coupon today!

Gold Eagle Reader Service, a division of Worldwide Library
In U.S.A.: 2504 W. Southern Avenue, Tempe, Arizona 85282
In Canada: 649 Ontario Street, Stratford, Ontario N5A 6W2

FREE! MACK BOLAN BUMPER STICKER
when you join our home subscription plan.

YES. please send me my first four Executioner novels. and include my FREE
Mack Bolan bumper sticker as a gift. These first four books are mine to examine free for
10 days. If I am not entirely satisfied with these books. I will return them within 10 days
and owe nothing. If I decide to keep these novels. I will pay just $1.95 per book (total
$7.80). I will then receive the four new Executioner novels every other month as soon
as they come off the presses. and will be billed the same low price of $7.80 per ship-
ment. I understand that each shipment will contain two Mack Bolan novels. one Able
Team and one Phoenix Force. There are no shipping and handling or any other hidden
charges. I may cancel this arrangement at any time. and the bumper sticker is mine to
keep as a FREE gift. even if I do not buy any additional books.

NAME _____
(PLEASE PRINT)

ADDRESS _____ APT. NO. _____

CITY _____ STATE/PROV. _____ ZIP/POSTAL CODE _____

Signature _____ (If under 18. parent or guardian must sign.)

This offer limited to one order per household. We reserve the right to exercise discretion in
granting membership. If price changes are necessary. you will be notified.

Offer expires August 31, 1983   166-BPM-PAB7